TAE KELLER

Illustrated by
GERALDINE RODRÍGUEZ

HENRY HOLT AND COMPANY
New York

Henry Holt and Company, *Publishers since 1866*
Henry Holt® is a registered trademark of Macmillan Publishing Group, LLC
120 Broadway, New York, NY 10271 • mackids.com

Our books may be purchased in bulk for promotional, educational, or business
use. Please contact your local bookseller or the Macmillan Corporate and
Premium Sales Department at (800) 221-7945 ext. 5442 or by email at
MacmillanSpecialMarkets@macmillan.com.

Library of Congress Control Number: 2022908222

First edition, 2022
Book design by Veronica Mang
Printed in the United States of America by Lakeside Book Company,
Harrisonburg, Virginia

ISBN 978-1-250-81431-9
1 3 5 7 9 10 8 6 4 2

For Sunhi—

who traveled with me into hidden worlds

and found magic

Homesick River

Wood of Nightmares

Treehouse
Village

Information
Booth

Healing
Orchard

Rainbow Forest

Just Right
Home Cottage

Sleeping Beauty's Castle

ஃ Chapter 1 ௬

ihi Whan Park was a princess.

Well, kind of.

To be more precise: Mihi Whan Park *felt* like a princess, like someone important, someone who mattered, someone who *belonged*—even if she hadn't quite found her palace yet. Deep in her heart, Mihi felt like long-lost royalty, born to a king and queen in a far-off fantasyland.

Of course, if you asked anyone else, they'd tell you Mihi was . . . just a girl. A four-foot-tall Korean girl, born to the owners of Park Pet Rescue in Medford, Massachusetts.

But those were pesky details.

Another pesky detail: Mihi's morning was not going as planned.

"Do we *really* have to play Snow White?" Genevieve Donnelly pouted as she twirled her blonde ponytail around her finger.

Genevieve was Mihi's best friend . . . ish. They'd been close since they were little, but lately, Genevieve didn't seem to *like* Mihi very much. And unfortunately, that was kind of a friendship requirement.

Mihi made herself smile, as if Genevieve were just joking around. "We played your game yesterday, so we're playing mine today."

They played together on the playground every morning before school, and before this year, they'd always played princesses. But lately . . .

Genevieve sighed the world's most dramatic sigh. "Fi-ine. Did you bring the apple?"

Mihi attempted to radiate pure sunshine to make up for Genevieve's rain cloud of a mood. "Of course!"

She swung her backpack off her shoulder and ruffled through crumpled worksheets and candy wrappers. "I definitely, one hundred percent, *know* I packed it."

Except, for reasons she could not comprehend, the apple wasn't there.

She thought back to this morning. She'd been holding the apple in her hand. She'd looked at her backpack. And she'd thought, very clearly: *Don't forget this!*

But she'd also been waiting downstairs while her parents got her little brother ready. And downstairs was her family's pet shelter.

Her parents had recently gotten some new birds after a family moved and needed to rehome them, and Mihi had looked at the creatures, trapped inside their cages.

Watching them, her heart had pinched. They'd seemed so *sad*. And sure, she knew her parents wouldn't be thrilled if she opened their cages, but the birds deserved freedom!

Mihi had imagined the result: The birds would dance around her and tweet their gratitude before flying out the open window. Then, every morning after that, they'd visit her window to help her get dressed.

But what *really* happened . . . wasn't that.

What *really* happened involved the chaotic flutter of sixteen panicked birds, five barking dogs, four meowing cats, and two very unhappy parents.

And during all of that, Mihi had forgotten the apple.

"Well, I guess we can't play." Genevieve shrugged like this was no big deal.

But for Mihi, it was. She already had the sick-making feeling that Genevieve wouldn't want to play princesses for much longer. And Mihi wasn't ready for that to end. This was the only chance Mihi got to imagine an impossibly magical life.

She had to get an apple.

An idea began to shimmer in Mihi's mind, and she pointed to the corner of the playground where a giant apple tree grew—an apple tree that they were definitely, 100 percent, totally and completely forbidden to climb. "We could get a *new* apple."

Genevieve frowned. "Mihi, that's a terrible idea."

"But—"

"Look, I'm not trying to be mean, but . . ." Genevieve took a deep breath. "I think it's time to stop playing princesses. It's babyish and kind of annoying, and the other kids think so, too, if you haven't noticed. You're not really the princess type anyway."

Mihi blinked.

"No offense," Genevieve added.

The worst part was Genevieve didn't look like she was trying to be mean. She just looked sad. Sad because Mihi didn't understand. Sad because she *pitied* Mihi. Genevieve was the type of girl who just, somehow, had all the answers—how to dress, how to act, how to matter in the world.

All Mihi had was questions.

"The princess type?" Mihi repeated, the words echoing in her head.

Genevieve's frown deepened. "Maybe you can find friends that match you better, like Amy Lee or Abbie Wu. And you can play . . . ninjas or something."

It was like Genevieve had started speaking a foreign language. Mihi felt the way she did when her grandparents spoke Korean. She could pick out some of the words, but she couldn't put them together in a way that made sense.

She frowned. "But I don't *know* Amy or Abbie. And I don't *like* ninjas. I like—" She stopped. She wasn't sure if she was about to say *princesses* or *you*. How horrible.

"It's just a suggestion," Genevieve said apologetically. Then she walked away, leaving Mihi in the middle of the playground.

All around her, other kids played with their friends, and Mihi just stood there, alone.

Hurt and embarrassment boiled in her chest, and she started sweating. Genevieve had been pulling away for a long time, but this was so much worse than Mihi had feared.

Genevieve's words dug deep—straight to the part of Mihi that wondered if they were true. It was like Genevieve had unlocked a secret fear, one that had hidden in Mihi's heart for so long: What if she wasn't good enough to be a princess?

Because the problem was, though Mihi *felt* like one, sometimes when she looked in the mirror—or worse, when someone like perfect, pretty Genevieve looked at her—that feeling disappeared. Mihi could only see her own round nose and rounder face. Her stick-straight hair and her sticking-out front teeth.

She could only see the too annoying, too chubby, too babyish girl that Genevieve didn't want to be friends with.

But no.

I can play Snow White if I want to, Mihi told herself, trying to believe it. *I am the princess type.*

Mihi's eyes fell back on that apple tree, and she gritted her teeth. "I'll show her," she murmured. Then she grabbed her backpack and marched over to the forbidden tree.

Chapter 2

Mihi wasn't planning to climb the tree. Not at first.

Positioning herself right below the most perfect apple, she closed one eye and made a box with her fingers, framing her goal. The leaves on the other trees were burnt orange and threatening to fall soon, but the apple tree stood big and bright with its shiny red fruit.

One apple, the biggest and brightest of all, called to her. That was the one.

She tapped her necklace, a golden crown pendant, for good luck. Then she lifted her backpack, took aim, and *threw*.

She envisioned what would happen next: Her bag would arc up, up, up, until it hit the perfect apple, knocking the fruit right into Mihi's outstretched hands.

But what *really* happened . . . wasn't that. In truth, Mihi had terrible aim.

She watched the backpack arc up, up, up, into the trees and then—stop. The backpack got stuck in the branches.

Oh. Hot tears pricked behind Mihi's eyes, which she hated. She felt like a little kid. *Babyish.*

She shook her head. She had to get that apple. She had to prove . . . well, she wasn't sure what, exactly. She just knew she had to get it.

Before she could stop herself, she was climbing— hand over hand, foot over foot. It was thrilling. She felt like maybe, just maybe, she could leave Genevieve's words behind.

Mihi had spent much of her life watching princess movies, so she knew there were different kinds of prin-cesses. There were the sleeping kind—the old movies. And then there were the prince-hunting kind. And then there were the newer princesses, the ones who went on epic journeys as the heroes of their own stories.

Mihi loved every princess, but she especially loved that last group, with Elsa, and Raya, and Rapunzel. Those princesses chased adventure and kept moving, kept *going*, until they achieved their dreams—until they became the people they were meant to be. Mihi would do that, too, until she had that perfect life where everything fit. Where *she* fit.

A happily ever after was out there for Mihi. She just had to find it.

Now, climbing like this, Mihi felt very regal. She imagined her hair blowing royally in the wind, even though she knew it was probably hanging limply. She imagined the sun peeking through the leaves, lighting her up like the chosen one.

She was getting closer and closer to that apple, and it was all going so well, really, until she heard a voice, slicing through her fantasy: "MIHI WHAN PARK."

Mihi winced as she looked down. She hadn't realized how high she'd climbed. Seeing the ground so far below her, her heart began to pound, and she felt a little woozy.

And there, back on Earth, beside a crowd of her

classmates, was Ms. George, the playground monitor, with her hands on her hips and her hair pulled into a tight bun. Even from this distance, Mihi could see her lips forming a thin line.

For the record, Mihi was not Ms. George's favorite student.

And for the record, Mihi was in trouble.

Chapter 3

Indoor recess.

This wasn't the first time one of Mihi's ideas had landed her there. But it wasn't so bad. Sure, it wasn't as good as being outside, but Mihi didn't exactly *want* to be outside anymore considering:

- Everyone was talking about her tree-climbing incident, and
- She was newly friendless.

Besides, the librarian, Ms. Lavender, usually gave Mihi candy. Honestly, she'd gotten off easy.

As Mihi walked past the front desk, Ms. Lavender looked up from her computer. She was pale, blue-eyed, and tiny—barely taller than Mihi—but her hair, piled on her head, added six inches. It should have been white, but she always dyed it lavender to match her name.

"Indoor recess again?" she asked, eyes crinkling as she smiled. "I heard about the tree."

Mihi sighed. "Genevieve told me I should stop playing princesses and I . . ." She stopped, deciding to leave out the "princess-type" part. "I had to prove her wrong."

"Oh, Mihi." Sympathy flooded Ms. Lavender's eyes. "Don't let anybody make you feel bad about loving fairy tales. You appreciate the classics. That's a good thing."

A smile tugged at Mihi's lips. Ms. Lavender always had a way of lifting her spirits. "And I don't mind indoor recess," Mihi added. "The library is nice."

"You always focus on the positive. That's what I love about you," the librarian said. "But as much as I enjoy seeing you, I don't want you breaking any more rules. And I don't want you putting yourself in danger."

Mihi nodded. As cool as Ms. Lavender was, she

was still an adult. Which meant she loved rules. "Yes, Ms. Lavender."

"Good. Now, I've got to make some photocopies in the teacher's lounge. Savannah Brown and Reese Baker are sitting at the back table, if you want to say hi. Don't cause any trouble while I'm gone." With a wink, she shuffled a stack of papers, stood up, and walked away.

Mihi made her way to the back of the library, toward the long table where kids sometimes gathered. Today Savannah sat at one end of the table, her hair falling into her face as she read a book in her lap. Reese sat at the other end, scribbling on a math worksheet.

They were all in the same grade, but they'd never been in the same class, so Mihi had never officially met them. All she knew about Savannah was that she seemed sweet, and quieter than the musical theater kids she usually hung out with. As for Reese, she was new this year and known for being super smart.

On any other day Mihi would've been excited to talk to new people, but today she thought of what Genevieve said, and her stomach clenched with nerves.

Would these girls find Mihi babyish and annoying too?

She gestured to a chair at the table. "Can I sit here?" she asked, hesitating just slightly.

Savannah looked up, giving the smallest of smiles as she pushed her light brown hair out of her green eyes.

At the sound of Mihi's voice, Reese jumped a bit, as if she'd been so absorbed in her equations that she hadn't noticed anyone else was around. "Of course you can," she said.

Mihi sat, and an awkward silence stretched between them. None of them could decide if they should go back to their own thing or make conversation.

Don't be annoying, Mihi reminded herself. She always tried too hard. That's what Genevieve used to say. She should keep quiet and let these girls be.

But . . . what if they wanted to be friends? "Reese and Savannah, right?" Mihi introduced herself. "It's really nice to meet you. I get indoor recess kind of a lot, but I'm usually in it alone."

"It's nice to meet you too," Reese said. And with that, the awkward silence snapped. Reese pushed her thick red glasses up her nose, and her dark brown eyes glittered with curiosity. "I heard you climbed the apple tree this morning. I'd estimate three feet between each branch, so that's impressive. How'd you get so high?"

Savannah leaned forward and whispered, with something close to awe, "You must have been so scared."

"A little," Mihi admitted. "But I had to get an apple." Before they could ask *why*, she changed the subject. "How'd you two get indoor recess?"

Reese exhaled a very long sigh. "The overhead projector in my class wasn't working, so I tried to fix it. I'm pretty good at fixing things. But when my teacher found me standing on a desk, examining the projector, she thought I was trying to steal it. So, here I am." She lifted her palms in a shrug, as if to say, *What can you do?* But Mihi could see the hurt in her eyes.

"But you were trying to help." Mihi paused. "And why would you even *want* a projector?"

That surprised a laugh out of Reese. "That's the real question, isn't it? But when I told my teacher I was trying to help, she didn't believe me."

"That's terrible," Savannah whispered, and Mihi nodded in agreement.

When Reese gave that *I-don't-care-but-I-do-care* shrug again, Savannah asked, "Where'd you learn to fix it?"

"I like to take things apart," Reese explained, "to see how they work. I used to take apart clocks and remote controls. Last year, I took apart my sister's Xbox—which got me grounded for a month."

"*Cool*," Savannah breathed. Mihi noticed that Savannah said everything with a hint of quiet wonder, like she was constantly surprised by the world. Mihi liked that.

"So, what about you? How'd you end up here?" Reese asked Savannah.

"Oh." Savannah blushed, her whole face and most of her neck going sunset pink. "I didn't do anything. Sometimes the library is just easier than outdoor recess. And I like to read." She held up a bright pink book. On the cover, a pretty blonde girl wore a crown and a ball gown.

Mihi blurted, "You like princess stories too?"

Savannah nodded enthusiastically.

Reese raised an eyebrow. "It's hard not to."

Mihi's heart spun in her chest. Somehow, she'd

ended up in indoor recess with two girls who seemed nice and interesting and *both loved princess stories.* This seemed beyond lucky. This seemed like . . . destiny.

And because of that, Mihi took a chance. She leaned forward and confessed the horrible fear in her heart, the one flamed by Genevieve's words. "I love them, too, but I'm not sure I'm the princess type."

Reese and Savannah were silent, and Mihi worried she'd made a terrible mistake. She shouldn't have told them. This wasn't something normal people felt.

But, finally, Savannah tugged at a strand of her hair, pulling it over her eye as she said, "Me neither."

"Same." Reese nodded. Just one simple word, but a sad one.

Mihi blinked. Reese was one of the few Black kids in school, and Mihi wondered if Reese felt the same way she sometimes did—like everyone else at school was laughing at a joke she hadn't heard the punchline to. Mihi was always trying to laugh along, hoping nobody noticed her confusion.

"Neither of you deserve to feel that way," Mihi told them. "You're both so nice." She looked at

Reese, with her dark curls and sparkling intelligence, and Savannah, with her wide green eyes and hopeful smile. They looked like birds had helped them get dressed in the morning—rather than flapping around them in total chaos.

Savannah's cheeks flushed, but she shook her head. "Thanks, but I'm not cut out to be the star of the show. And I don't like princes. I'd rather end up with— well, I'd rather end up alone in a castle, with flowers and a fish."

Reese laughed, before clapping a hand over her mouth. "Sorry. Most of that makes sense. But . . . a fish?"

"Cats and dogs are scary." Savannah blushed again, and Mihi wondered if she got dizzy with all the blood rushing to and from her face. "They can bite, which is dangerous. But fish are safe. And they're covered in slime that helps them move through water, which is neat."

"Slime is cool," Mihi said, because it was.

Savannah nodded, and silence stretched around them until Reese lifted her shoulders, scrunching them up to her ears. "The only Black princess is a frog."

"True." Savannah winced, and then added, as if it was the only thing she could think to say, "Did you know that some frogs have slime that kills the flu?"

Reese opened and closed her mouth like she had no idea how to respond. Then she snorted. "Well, at least there's that."

Mihi felt a tug toward these girls, a feeling like this could be the start of a real friendship.

And then there it was again: the shimmer of a new idea. A way to *bond*. Nothing bonded people quite like an adventure.

She lowered her voice. "Have you had Ms. Lavender's candy before?"

Savannah sat up straighter. "Of course! She gives them to us at the end of library period. They're the most delicious candies I've ever tasted."

Savannah was right. Ms. Lavender's hard candies seemed to catch rainbows in the light, and they tasted like color itself.

Reese bobbed her head in agreement.

Mihi grinned. "What if we snuck into Ms. Lavender's lounge?"

Savannah frowned. "Won't we get in trouble? We're not allowed in there."

Reese and Savannah exchanged a glance, and worry flashed in Mihi's chest—fear that she'd made a mistake, that she'd lose these friends before she even made them. But this was a *good* idea. A nice, simple one, where nothing could possibly go wrong. "Ms. Lavender went to photocopy some papers, but we can tell her when she gets back," Mihi insisted.

Reese considered this. "I don't think she'd mind. She's always giving kids candy."

Savannah weighed the consequences in her head, and Mihi expected her to say no. But then she chewed her lip and nodded, making her decision with the hint of a smile. "Okay, let's do it."

"Perfect." Mihi beamed. She'd known this was a good plan.

With renewed energy, the girls bounced to their feet and hurried into their librarian's lounge.

It was a small space, no bigger than a bathroom, with just a tiny cabinet and a refrigerator. On the wall hung a handful of framed photos: Ms. Lavender with her children and grandchildren. Ms. Lavender with her siblings. And a faded photo of two girls, arms wrapped around one another, wearing big smiles and plastic gold crowns. It took Mihi a moment to recognize the young Ms. Lavender. Seeing the librarian as a kid made Mihi like her even more, but there wasn't time to admire photos. They were on a mission.

Reese pulled the refrigerator door open, and there, sitting on an otherwise empty shelf, was a mountain of candy. Wrapped in pink foil, the candies shimmered, inviting them to taste.

"They're so pretty," Savannah breathed.

Mihi took two pieces and dropped them into Reese's and Savannah's hands. "Your candy," she said, bowing as if they were royalty. Laughing, they unwrapped their pieces.

Mihi took one for herself and enjoyed the musical sound of crinkling foil as she opened it. Pocketing the wrapper, she

closed her eyes and popped the candy into her mouth. Sugar flooded her system.

"It tastes like the red bean rice cakes my mom makes," Mihi murmured.

"It tastes like buttercream frosting," Reese said.

"I think it tastes like beef jerky," Savannah said. "Which is delicious."

Normally Mihi would have wondered how the candy tasted so different to each of them, but she was too busy savoring the flavor—until Savannah gasped. "Are you seeing this?"

Mihi opened her eyes.

She'd expected to see the inside of the refrigerator again—the glow of the light, the white plastic shelves, the pile of candy, and a few cans of diet soda.

But now when Mihi looked into the refrigerator, she saw . . . trees.

She saw a *forest*.

And not just any forest, but a rainbow-coated one, with pastel-streaked tree trunks and neon leaves. A layer of dark purple moss covered the ground, looking soft as velvet, and everything glowed with warm sunlight.

This place . . .

This place was . . . *not the inside of a refrigerator.*

Mihi blinked hard, but nothing changed. She slammed the refrigerator door closed. Then cracked it open again.

Still forest.

Gulping, Mihi pushed the door shut.

The three girls stared at each other. Nobody knew what to say.

Reese cleared her throat. "That's unusual."

Savannah tugged at her hair. Mihi stared at the fridge.

And then, all at once, the three of them reached for the handle again, pulling the door back open.

There it was. The rainbow forest.

"It smells like rain," Savannah murmured.

Mihi leaned forward as far as she dared. It seemed as if she could step right through that refrigerator, onto the moss in front of her.

"But this doesn't make sense," Reese said, as she

dropped to her knees and inspected the back of the refrigerator. "This is impossible."

Those words lifted the hairs on Mihi's neck. "*Impossible*," she whispered. The word tasted like adventure.

"We should probably tell Ms. Lavender," Savannah said.

But it was too late. Mihi had already stepped through.

Chapter 4

Yes, confirmed: Mihi was not inside a refrigerator. She was very much in a forest.

Mud squelched up around her white sneakers as her shoes sank into the moss. A slight breeze lifted Mihi's hair. This felt like . . . magic.

From behind her, Mihi heard Reese's voice, tight with disbelief. "This can't be happening."

And then Savannah's, dipped in panic. "*What* is happening?"

"You followed!" Mihi felt a heart-burst of relief as she turned to see them. Savannah clung to Reese's arm and frowned at the ground beneath her, as if it might swallow her up.

To be fair, it *might*. The universe wasn't exactly behaving as usual today.

Reese shook her head, shoving her glasses up her nose. "This completely defies the laws of nature."

"We are way past the laws of nature," Savannah responded, eyes wide.

But Mihi was only half listening, because she was focused on what was behind them.

Or rather, what *wasn't* behind them.

All around, the colorful forest sprawled and stretched—but the refrigerator was nowhere to be found.

"Um . . ." Mihi murmured, pointing to where the refrigerator *should* have been. Suddenly, the breeze felt a bit too cold. Mihi shivered.

Savannah squeaked. "There's no door. Oh no oh no ohno. We'regonnadie."

"We are not gonna die." Mihi tried to sound reassuring. "I'm sure there's a way back."

But as Mihi tried to think of a way back, her mind went blank and terror crept in. Magic was amazing. But magic without a way home was . . . less amazing.

"Look at this." Reese held up her shimmering candy wrapper, tilting it left and right. "Do your wrappers have writing on them?"

Mihi leaned forward to see the little trees drawn on Reese's wrapper. Except those trees weren't staying still. They seemed to sway, like they were dancing in an invisible breeze. Beneath the trees, a scrawl of text appeared: *The Rainbow Forest*.

"That must be where we are!" Mihi said.

Glancing around, Savannah whispered, "How does it know where we are?"

Mihi pulled her own candy wrapper from her pants pocket and smoothed the crumpled foil. Though it had been blank before, her wrapper now contained a piece of a map: a long rippling river dotted with small cottages, leading all the way to a castle.

A *castle*.

If this forest was real, that castle must be real too. Mihi looked up at the sugar-soaked trees around her, excitement and fear fighting for control of her heart. Was this really happening?

Savannah held up her wrapper-map. On it, cursive labels shimmered to the surface: *The Healing Orchard. The Village. The Information Booth.* The map shook in her trembling hands.

Reese pointed to *The Information Booth* and said, "That's where we need to go. The more we know, the better we can strategize. Do you think this is some kind of virtual reality?" She walked over to a tree and knocked three times on the wood. The wood knocked back.

Reese stumbled backward, tensing for something terrible to happen, but the tree just stood there, as if it were a totally normal, rainbow-colored knocking tree.

"Okay," Mihi agreed. "We need to get from the Rainbow Forest on Reese's map to the Information Booth on Savannah's map."

Reese leaned over, lining her piece up with Savannah's, and as soon as the maps touched, they glowed bright and began to stitch together. Mihi aligned hers and the girls watched as all their wrappers became a single shimmering map.

"*Wow*," Savannah breathed, fear momentarily forgotten.

"Now *that* was magical," Mihi said.

"Magic is impossible," Reese reminded them.

Mihi grinned. That was exactly the point.

Chapter 5

They followed a winding stone path through the woods, and Mihi basked in the magic of the forest. Where she walked, the grass bent a path for her, as if it had been expecting her. As if it were bowing to her.

When she ran her hand over a tree trunk, the bark purred like a cat.

And once, when Mihi looked at the sky, she could have sworn one of the clouds bent and pulled into the word *Howdy* before drifting apart and blowing into mist.

So yes, they needed to find a way out of here. But the more Mihi saw of the forest, the less she wanted to leave it. How could a place so impossibly incredible be dangerous?

Eventually, their path ended at a huge tree with

long, low-hanging branches. From each branch dangled brightly colored scarves and silver wind chimes that sang in the breeze.

Reese consulted the map. "Well, we're here, though I don't feel more informed."

Circling the tree, Savannah called out, "I think I found something?"

When Reese and Mihi walked around to join her, Mihi sucked in a breath.

The center of the tree had been carved out. Inside the hollow were three dollhouses: one yellow, one blue, one pink and bedazzled. Light flickered behind the windows, as if miniature fireplaces blazed inside.

"What—" Mihi began to ask, but before the question left her lips, a grey mouse wearing round glasses and a pinstripe suit stepped out of the yellow house. Oblivious to the girls, the mouse walked over to its miniature mailbox and began sorting through its mail.

Reese leaned forward until her nose nearly touched the mouse's back, and examined the creature as it shuffled through tiny envelopes. "It looks so *real*," she murmured.

Having gathered all its mail, the mouse spun around—and came nose-to-nose with Reese.

"AHHHH!" The mouse threw its arms up, scattering mail into the air.

Reese stepped back. "Sorry! Sorry! I didn't mean—" Then she turned to Mihi and Savannah and shook her head with disbelief. "I'm apologizing to a *mouse*."

"I'm sure this will all make sense in a minute," Mihi said, though she wasn't sure it would. And she wasn't sure she wanted it to.

Grabbing the mailbox for support, the mouse took deep breaths, attempting to recover from its minor heart attack. "What—ah—ahem—what brings you here?"

Savannah's eyebrows skyrocketed. "The mouse *talks?*"

Reese eyed the creature suspiciously, like it was a robot that might explode. Savannah took three steps back, like it might morph into a giant alligator and swallow her whole.

Mihi said, carefully, "We're lost."

The mouse cleared its throat. "You're not lost. You're at the Information Booth."

Mihi hesitated. "Yes. But, well, we were hoping you could tell us what this place . . . *is?*"

"And how it works," Reese added.

"And how to get back home," Savannah reminded them.

The pin-striped mouse tilted its head, as if *they* were the strange ones. "I'm afraid I don't understand."

The blue door banged open and a second mouse stepped out—this one in a silver floor-length gown and cat-eye glasses. "Jonathan, what are you—ohhh." Her nose twitched. "How interesting."

"They say they're lost," Jonathan informed the new mouse.

She grinned, and Mihi noticed her teeth were sharp. Did all mice have such sharp teeth? "Well, of course they're lost," the mouse said. "They're from the Grey World."

Jonathan shook his head. "Misty, you can't believe that. Those doors were destroyed a long time ago."

"Oh, I believe it." Misty took a step forward. "I can smell it."

Mihi took a step back. Mice in fairy tales weren't

usually dangerous, but after being attacked by a mouse at the shelter, Mihi didn't trust them. And besides, her world wasn't *grey*. It might not be as colorful as this—but still! "We're not from a grey world," she informed them. "We're from Medford."

"How delightful." Misty laughed a wind-chime laugh. "It talks."

Now Savannah cleared her throat, her hair falling over her face. "Um, yes, we do . . . talk. And if you could help us get home, we'd be so grateful."

Jonathan shuddered. "You want to go back *there?*"

"Yes," Reese said. "To Medford. In Massachusetts. Not to that grey world or wherever."

Misty nodded sympathetically. "Yes, yes. Medford sounds lovely, in a dreadfully dull kind of way. We *can* help you return, if you insist. But perhaps you'd like to consider the alternatives?"

"Alternatives?" Mihi repeated. Before she could form a full question, the forest suddenly filled with swirling lights and a deep musical beat.

The *entire* forest.

It was like someone had flipped off the sun and turned on a disco ball.

The girls inched closer to one another, wide-eyed with fear and wonder and . . . confusion.

"Introduuuucing . . ." A deep voice boomed around them, but Mihi couldn't tell where it was coming from. "The one, the on-lyyy . . ."

Jonathan rubbed his temples like he had a headache.

"HOU-DI-NIIIII!!" The door to the pink house burst open and a third mouse stepped through. This white mouse was the biggest of the three, wearing diamond-encrusted glasses and a sequined jacket.

"Why yes, hello, Houdini, welcome to the party," Misty sighed. "We haven't got all day. These are Greys. They don't know how they got here."

"We actually got here through a refri—" Mihi began, but Reese elbowed her into silence and Mihi clamped her lips shut. Reese was right: Now was probably not the time to blurt out whatever came to mind.

A small smile spread across the white mouse's face. "Ah, Greys. I didn't think I'd ever see one again."

"Sure, it's all quite amazing." Misty waved a paw like Houdini's interest bored her. "Explain the situation and let's figure out what to do with them."

"Of course. Pleased to make your acquaintance . . ."
Houdini gestured to Mihi, waiting for her name.

"Mi—Mihi. Mihi Whan Park."

"Mihi Whan Park," Houdini repeated. He reached
for her pointer finger, knelt, and kissed her nail.

Mihi tried not to shudder.

"Mihi, Reese, and Savannah of Medford," Houdini
announced, after Reese and Savannah also introduced
themselves, "you know us by many names. Perhaps
you recognize us as the mice who rescued Princess Cinderella."

Mihi gasped. "Cinderella's mice!"

"You help a human *one time* and they think they
own you," Misty drawled.

Houdini continued, "Or you may know us from that highly unfortunate rhyme—"

"The Three Blind Mice," Savannah whispered. "Like the nursery rhyme."

"No," Misty bit out. "*Not* like the nursery rhyme."

Savannah paled.

"We are not blind," Jonathan corrected. "We are *nearsighted*."

Houdini cleared his throat. "But our true name is the Great Mice, three of the most powerful creatures in this world. We know all. We know your future. We know your *destiny*." On the last word, he did jazz hands for dramatic effect.

"Destiny," the girls repeated.

Reese frowned in disbelief. Savannah's eyes grew wide.

And Mihi . . . fought back a smile. She couldn't help it.

Destiny.

Jonathan sighed. "Houdini, you make us sound like fortune-tellers. In reality, we're—"

"Both feared and revered throughout the land," Misty finished.

"I was going to say we're more like file keepers," Jonathan said. "But okay."

Houdini continued as if they hadn't spoken. "As the *greatest* mouse,"—Misty scoffed, but Houdini ignored her—"I am about to tell you something that will change your lives forever."

Savannah reached over and grabbed Mihi's hand, her grip so tight Mihi thought it might cut off her circulation. But instead of pulling away, Mihi squeezed back. She had the overwhelming feeling that her fate had finally found her.

"All the fairy tales you've heard are real," Houdini said. "And somehow, the three of you have made your way inside them."

Chapter 6

"We're inside the fairy tales?" Mihi breathed. "For real?"

"As real as fire-breathing dragons, evil witches, and fairy godmothers," Misty responded.

A fairy *godmother*? Mihi tried not to squeal. *Play it cool, Mihi. Play it cool.*

Houdini clapped his paws together. "Welcome to the Rainbow Realm! So, what do you say? Would you like to spend a little time here? We can send you right home as soon as you're bored."

Mihi's spine tingled with temptation. This. This was beyond anything she'd ever imagined. This was everything she'd ever wanted.

Savannah chewed her cheek. "Our teachers will worry. And our *parents*."

She was right. If only they'd been able to leave a note. But what would it have said? *We're headed off to a fairy-tale world. Back in a few days! Ta-ta!*

Jonathan cleared his throat. "Not a concern. If you need the Grey World to wait for you, it will. Time passes differently here."

"Fairy tales are *timeless*, darling," Misty said. She sounded like one of those old-fashioned actresses in the movies Mihi's grandmother watched to practice English. Mihi would curl up with her grandmother on the couch while a white-haired starlet flitted across the screen like the whole world belonged to her.

"No one will notice you're gone," Houdini confirmed.

A twinge of homesickness flared in Mihi's chest, but she squashed it. Houdini was right; no one would notice. Her family was too busy with the pet rescue. The kids at school mostly ignored her or gave her awkward glances. Her teachers just sighed.

At home, Mihi was nobody. But here . . .

Reese crossed her arms, doubtful. "So we've managed to bend both space *and* time?"

"It's magic," Mihi insisted. "We could explore our favorite stories. We could meet our favorite characters. We could have an adventure."

Then she stopped, an idea forming. She turned to the mice. "Could *we* be princesses?"

Misty wind-chime laughed. "Ridiculous."

But Houdini thought for a moment. "Now that's interesting."

Jonathan's mouth fell open. "Hou-*di*-ni. That is not—"

"Jonathan," Houdini interrupted. "We haven't seen Greys in so long. Why can't we have a little fun?"

Misty grinned, her sharp teeth flashing. "Fun," she repeated, in a way that made the hairs on Mihi's arms prickle. "With the Greys."

"Oh, Misty. Don't be so frightening." Houdini turned to the girls and explained, "Back in the old days, the veil between our world and the Greys' was as thin as the breeze. But as the years went on, your world shifted. It grew more complicated, and your people grew fearful. They feared change, and the strange, and most of all, they feared magic. So they built a wall between worlds and slammed the door shut."

Mihi's heart crumpled as she imagined the world before—an open door between reality and fairy tale, fantasy smudged into a blurry line, a world where anything was possible.

And then, all of that gone—the door to dreams slammed shut.

Houdini continued, "All they had left of us were their memories, so they told stories about us. Of course, they got some things wrong. They embellished. They overlooked."

Jonathan huffed. *"Three blind mice."*

"You understand why *some* of us 'Bows think poorly of Greys," Houdini continued. "But not us! That is water under a bridge, as your people say!"

"So . . ." Savannah hesitated. "Is this realm really full of scary, dangerous things?"

"Well, a little, of course," Houdini confessed. "I'm sure you've heard the stories. But it's full of delightful magic as well. *We,* dare I say it, are delightful."

Savannah grimaced.

"But we'd keep you safe. Nothing is going to hurt you here," Houdini said.

Misty flashed a grin. "As long as you stay out of the Wood of Nightmares."

Savannah looked like she might pass out.

Mihi cleared her throat. She wished Misty would go away. Speaking to Houdini only, she asked, "So, you'd let us create our own fairy tales?"

"Ah, sure!" The bedazzled mouse spread his arms. "Sure! You can train to be princesses, and if you succeed, you can have your very own fairy tale. Then, when it's over, you can go home whenever you'd like."

Mihi glanced at her friends. Reese narrowed her eyes. Savannah twisted her hands together.

Houdini said, "I'm sure you've dreamt of it. You could be everything a princess is. Brilliant—"

Reese inhaled.

"—and beloved . . ."

Savannah chewed her cheek.

"You could belong," the mouse finished.

Mihi's heart grew wings.

She pulled Reese and Savannah into a huddle. "What do you think?" she asked, hoping beyond hope that the answer was *of course*.

Reese bit her lip. Mihi could practically see her brain whirring. "I don't understand how any of this works. I'm not sure if we're in a parallel universe, or a virtual reality, or an elaborate hoax. But I'd like to figure it out, so I vote to explore. There's a lot we might be able to learn here. And if we can be princesses . . ." She paused, like she was trying not to get her hopes up. "I mean, that would be cool."

Genevieve's words swam up in Mihi's memory, and her heart gave a little *hmph*. Genevieve didn't know anything about the world, clearly. "We can prove we're the princess type, once and for all. I vote yes," Mihi said. "I vote a million yeses."

Reese fought back a smile. "Well, you only get one yes. We all have to agree. Savannah?"

Savannah looked down. Her hair fell over her face. "I don't know."

Mihi blinked away a sudden rush of tears. Savannah was going to say no. They were so *close*, so close to everything Mihi had ever dreamt of. Her throat went scratchy, but she refused to cry. "Please," she whispered.

To Mihi's surprise, Savannah lifted her face, and though she still spoke quietly, something sparked in her eyes. "Okay. As long as we go home right after, as long as our parents won't worry, and as long as we stay out of that nightmare wood . . . I'm in."

Relief rushed up fast and hard and Mihi threw her arms around Savannah, squeezing tight. Then she turned back to the mice and told them, in her most serious, important voice, "We would like to be princesses."

"I knew you would." Houdini's eyes glinted behind his glasses. "Now, let's discuss payment."

Mihi paused. The mouse wanted payment? "But, I thought us becoming princesses was just for fun."

Misty laughed. "And payment is *great* fun."

"Nothing unreasonable," Houdini insisted. "But we're giving you this opportunity, and we'd like a little something in exchange. Something interesting from the Grey World. We're collectors, after all."

The girls hesitated.

"You could have my . . ." Reese thought for a moment. "Watch?"

Misty sniffed. "No offense, love. But that's a bit drab for my taste."

Reese frowned, and Mihi whispered, "*I* like your watch."

"I have, uh, a scrunchie?" Savannah offered, pulling it off her wrist.

Jonathan sighed, like he couldn't believe he had to explain this. "Mice have no need for *scrunchies*."

Savannah frowned.

Mihi dug through her pockets, but all she found was lint.

"What about that?" Houdini said, eyeing Mihi's neck.

She touched her collarbone and found her crown pendant. But *no*. She couldn't give it up. It was her most precious possession. A gift from her mom. "This? Are you sure? It's probably too . . . drab for you."

"Not at all." Misty's nose twitched. "That has memories. I can sense it."

"And memories are very valuable to us." Houdini nodded.

Mihi squeezed the pendant. She loved it. But . . . this dream was worth it, wasn't it?

With a deep breath, Mihi unclasped her necklace and placed it in Houdini's waiting paws.

"*Perfect.*" Houdini grinned, and Mihi noticed, just briefly, that his teeth were rather sharp too. "Unfortunately, Greys are incapable of teleporting—condolences about that, by the way—so you'll have to walk. Follow this path on your map, and do not stray from it. Not all of this forest is safe for unsuspecting Greys, and not everyone will be as helpful as us."

When he waved a paw, the map vibrated in Mihi's hands. She looked down to see a glowing path etched into the wrapper. It curled through the woods, past a village and an orchard, and stopped at the castle.

"When you reach the castle, you will meet Sleeping Beauty's head lady-in-waiting," Houdini said. "She's a good friend of mine. And she will make all your dreams come true."

❧ Chapter 7 ❧

Sleeping Beauty. They were going to meet *Sleeping Beauty.* Though it wasn't Mihi's favorite fairy tale (it obviously fell into the "sleeping" category of princess stories), it was the first one she'd ever seen.

She remembered sitting with her mother on the couch, watching the blonde beauty light up their small TV. Her little brother had yawned and said this was the most boringest movie *ever,* but Mihi had been enchanted. Staring up at the screen, she'd thought, *That's who I'm supposed to be.*

Now, bubbles of excitement rose in Mihi's chest as she, Reese, and Savannah made their way along Houdini's path. Mihi could practically hear the triumphant music swelling in the background.

"Look at us," she started to sing. "Look where we are. In a fairy tale—a very fairy—"

"What are you doing?" Reese interrupted.

Mihi frowned. "I'm singing a princess song."

Savannah tilted her head. "I've never heard that song."

"Because it's a new one. I'm starting my own song. If we're in our own fairy tale, we should have a special song."

Reese's lips twitched. An almost smile. "Mihi, as much as I'd love to hear the rest of that song, I would like to remind you that this isn't a magical fairy-tale land. Because magic isn't real."

Mihi didn't understand why Reese couldn't believe. It was almost like she didn't *want* to believe. She nudged Reese. "Come on, you know you want to sing your own princess song."

"If you insist." Reese raised a brow, then took a deep breath. "Look at us. Look at where we are. In a world that . . . must have a perfectly logical explanation."

"Reese!" Mihi protested. "That doesn't even rhyme!"

"And yet it is true."

Mihi laughed. "Okay, *fiiine*. Savannah, your turn."

Savannah bit her lip and let her hair fall over her eyes. Her shoulders curled inward. "I don't sing."

Savannah's words were so heavy and final that Mihi's heart crunched. How horribly sad, not to sing. Mihi opened her mouth to ask why, but Reese gave a quick shake of her head, and Mihi dropped the subject. Maybe it wasn't her business.

"Well, anyway," Mihi said, trying to keep the tone light. According to Houdini's trail on the map, they should have reached a small village by now, and Mihi was beginning to worry. But she cleared her throat, continuing the conversation as if everything were fine. "It's fun to think about being princesses."

"Do you really think it's possible?" Savannah asked, as she climbed over a purple tree root. "To star in our very own fairy tale?"

"Of course," Mihi responded. "Anything can happen here. This place is magic."

"*Magic*," Savannah whispered, and Mihi couldn't tell if Savannah was hopeful or frightened. Maybe a bit of both. Admittedly, Mihi also felt a bit of both.

"Magic isn't real," Reese said automatically, just

as a tiny bluebird swooped in front of them and winked before flitting away.

Mihi turned back to Reese. "Exhibit A," she said.

Reese chewed her lip, but before she could provide a *perfectly logical explanation*, Savannah looked up and murmured, "*Oh.*"

Mihi followed her gaze. Above them, tucked among the trees, was a whole village. Nestled between the branches were about twenty different houses—but these were nothing like the white houses Mihi was used to in Medford.

These were treehouses. But that didn't quite do them justice either. Genevieve had a treehouse: a small wooden house balanced in an oak tree, painted white to match her actual house.

But unlike Genevieve's treehouse, these didn't look like somebody shrank a suburban home and stuck it inside a tree. These looked like they were part of the trees themselves. Their walls seemed to be made of carved wood and vines as colorful as the forest around them. Leaves burst from windows, and soft layers of moss covered the roofs.

"I've never seen anything like this," Reese breathed, abandoning her skepticism for a moment.

"We have to keep going," Mihi said, but even as the words left her lips she felt a tug toward one of the treehouses in particular. It was nestled into a big apple tree, one with gnarled, knotted branches, and the front door was painted bloodred. It looked enchanting and magical, just like everything else they'd seen—but there was something more, a little twist in her chest that said: *There's a story here.*

"How much farther?" Savannah asked, lifting Mihi from her thoughts. Mihi looked down at the map. Just ahead was an orchard, and after that, the castle. They were almost there.

Focus, Mihi reminded herself.

With some effort, she pulled herself away from the village in the trees and kept moving, farther down the path. The more distance they put between themselves and the village, the better Mihi felt. There was something strange about that place.

They emerged from the forest into a large field, and Reese pointed ahead. "There's the orchard."

Sure enough, there was a cluster of trees in the

middle of the field, blocked off by a wooden fence. The scent of fresh fruit filled the air, and Mihi grinned as she walked up to the tall rock wall. Above the rocks, she saw a burst of colorful leaves and branches peeking over the edge.

Embedded in the wall was a locked steel gate with an inscription carved into it.

"The Healing Orchard," Mihi read aloud. "Find here a cure for anything: illness, heartbreak, and nightmares."

Savannah took a step closer, thought better of it, then stepped back. "Do you think it can really cure anything?"

"Of course not," Reese said. She was sounding less and less sure of this though. She glanced back at the orchard, shaking her head slowly. "This . . . place. Where are we?"

Mihi wanted those answers too. But now, in the distance, she could see the faintest outline of a castle.

Or rather: In the distance, Mihi saw the faintest outline of her destiny.

They were close. They were so, so close.

Mihi began to run.

Chapter 8

The closer Mihi got, the larger it loomed—the castle, her dream—surrounded by rolling, flower-filled hills.

Mihi sprinted past all of it until, finally, she stopped in front of the castle doors. She felt dizzy. Her breath caught with both wonder and exertion, and she forced herself to breathe while Reese and Savannah caught up.

Remember this moment, she told herself. *This is your last moment as Just Mihi. Soon you will be Princess Mihi.*

"So, this is an actual fairy-tale castle?" Savannah asked, coming up behind her.

"Maybe," Reese said.

"Definitely," Mihi insisted.

Together, they pushed the heavy front doors open to reveal a grand marble ballroom with a golden staircase that spiraled around it—all the way up to a jewel-encrusted door.

Above them, hanging by what looked like a single thread, was a chandelier, its prisms casting rainbows across the room. Splashed across the walls was a colorful mural of the castle itself. Beneath the painted castle read the words: *Home is where the heart is.*

Mentally, Mihi tested the idea. Could this castle be her home?

She felt another twinge of homesickness, and this one was harder to ignore. Already, Mihi missed her family. She missed her mother's red bean rice cakes, her grandfather's cheesy puns, the chaos of too many animals, and even her little brother constantly getting better grades than her.

What would her family say if they could see her now? The morning after she'd watched the *Sleeping Beauty* movie for the first time, Mihi told her mom she wanted to be a princess, and though her mom seemed relieved that Mihi had developed a more *normal* interest than hunting for potato bugs in the park, sadness had passed across her face. Mihi never really understood it.

Now, though, she shoved those thoughts aside. This was a different world. She'd go home soon enough, but here she could make her dreams come true.

"Can you imagine *living* here?" Savannah whispered into Mihi's ear. "This place is beautiful."

"How does the chandelier hang like that?" Reese added, with awe. "It looks impossible."

Mihi felt a crunch of fondness. Who else, standing in *Sleeping Beauty's ballroom*, would notice the mechanics of a chandelier?

"Welcome, welcome." A shrill voice echoed off the gold and marble, and a tall woman entered the room. She smelled like sharp, minty toothpaste. And she didn't sound particularly welcoming. "You must be the girls Houdini told me about. My name is Bertha. I am Sleeping Beauty's head lady-in-waiting, and I oversee every single person in this castle."

"Really?" Mihi blurted. "I don't remember you from Sleeping Beauty's story."

Bertha's gaze turned icy, and she spoke—each—word very crisply. "I'll have you know: I run this place. It's a heavy workload, as you might imagine, which is why I'm *thrilled* to be managing . . ." She consulted the clipboard in her hands. "Mihi, Reese, and Savannah."

Bertha did not sound thrilled.

Her grey hair was pulled into a tight bun and her thin lips stretched into a sliver. When her blue eyes narrowed, Bertha reminded Mihi of someone, but she couldn't remember who.

"If you really want to be *princesses*," Bertha began, voice dripping with disapproval, "you must follow the rules. Number one: Do not speak to Sleeping Beauty. Your training will be in this castle, but you are not to interact with her. I, of course, know how her story goes, and it is my job to facilitate her happy ending. But as the hero of her story, she does not know anything about it, and it's very important to keep it that way. Do. Not. Enter." Bertha pointed to the jeweled door at the top of the staircase, and Mihi felt an electric bolt of excitement. That must be Sleeping Beauty's room! A real fairy-tale princess! Only a few steps away!

"*Sleeping Beauty!*" she mouthed to Reese and Savannah.

Frowning, Bertha continued. "Rule number two: Do not change this story in any way. You are not to interfere. Do you understand?"

The girls nodded.

Bertha pursed her lips. "If you are successful in your training, then we will find an ideal environment for Mihi and Reese."

"Environment?" Reese repeated.

"What about me?" Savannah asked.

"You, of course, will fit somewhere like this," Bertha told Savannah, gesturing to the grand castle.

"Really?" Savannah flushed, looking pleased.

"Oh, I'd like a castle too," Mihi said. She pictured herself twirling through the grand ballroom.

"You don't get to choose," Bertha said, and for a moment Mihi thought she saw a flash of genuine sympathy in Bertha's eyes. But just as quickly, it was gone, replaced with an expression so cold that Mihi knew she must have imagined it. "I don't make the rules, but I do enforce them."

Mihi bit her lip. Rules didn't sound like adventure.

"Not to worry though," Bertha continued. "There

are lots of wonderful places for you. I could see you in a world with ancient kingdoms, ancestors, and traditions."

Mihi frowned. She didn't *want* to be in an ancient kingdom. That sounded like Mulan, who was cool and all, but everyone always expected Mihi to be Mulan. She wanted to be someone new, someone different.

Doubt floated up inside her, but she knew the details shouldn't matter. One way or another, she would be a princess.

"Now, where was I before you so rudely interrupted?" Bertha cleared her throat. "Ah, yes, your individual training. Mihi will come with me to study fainting."

"Fainting?" Mihi asked. "Aren't there more important things to learn?"

Bertha's thin lips got even thinner. "That brings me to the final and most important rule. Rule number three: No asking questions."

She had so very *many*, but Mihi swallowed and nodded.

"There is a lot to learn," Bertha said. "And you will

learn it, in time. Soon enough, you will know everything you need to know in order to live as a princess."

Mihi shivered. This would all be worth it in the end. Her happily ever after. She looked at her friends, and despite Bertha's frostiness, they seemed excited too.

"Savannah," Bertha continued, "you will practice singing to animals."

Savannah's eyes widened. "Oh, no, I don't si—"

"And, Reese," Bertha went on, silencing Savannah with a glare, "you will learn to identify curses."

"Wait," Reese blurted. "We'll be separated?"

"No questions," Bertha scolded, before reluctantly explaining. "Occasionally, you will participate in training activities together, for efficiency purposes, but for the most part you'll be on your own. And you should get used to that. A princess does not have time for *friends*. Animal sidekicks, yes. A prince, maybe. But friends . . ." She gave them a pointed look and shook her head. "Too distracting."

Savannah blinked. "But after training we'll get to be princesses *together*, right?"

"Of course not," Bertha replied. "After all, this is a competition."

The girls exchanged a startled glance, and Mihi's stomach tightened. No, no. This was her *dream*. This was her destiny. It had to include *friends*.

Bertha reached into the pockets of her dress and handed out three pins. They were round and flat, heavy and bronze. Mihi ran her thumb along the cold blank surface.

"Wear them," Bertha commanded.

"What are they?" Reese asked.

But when Bertha glared, the girls fastened the pins to their clothes without waiting for an answer. Mihi jabbed the sharp needle through her sweater, and stuck the backing onto the other side. The last time she'd worn a pin was when her family went to Disney World six years ago. There, she'd collected as many princess-themed pins as she could. Now, that memory seemed so far away.

As soon as the pin was fastened to her shirt, the blank surface began to swirl. Mihi sucked in a breath as she watched a big zero appear, right in the center.

"Only one of you can be a princess," Bertha explained. "These pins will record your scores, and whoever demonstrates the best ability during training will get her own story."

"What?" Dread pumped through Mihi's veins. This couldn't be right. "But—"

Bertha pursed her lips. "I thought you understood, but if you cannot handle it, you may leave."

"N-no," Mihi stammered. "It's fine. We'll do whatever we have to." The words were out of her mouth before she could stop them. Because they couldn't leave *now*. And surely once they showed

Bertha how great they *all* were, Bertha would change her mind. If not, Mihi would talk to Houdini, who seemed reasonable enough. He would help them.

Savannah looked at Mihi with panic in her eyes. Reese looked at Mihi with betrayal in hers.

"It'll be okay. I'll figure it out," Mihi whispered. But before she could explain any further, Bertha clapped her hands and waved for Mihi to follow.

Mihi hesitated for just a moment.

And then she followed. Alone.

Chapter 9

After two whole days of princess training, Mihi was *exhausted*. Who knew fainting required so much practice? But it was the good kind of exhaustion, because her days were packed with so much learning. She'd tried on ball gowns, tasted delicious cakes, and learned all the rules of princesshood.

There were rather . . . a lot of rules. But maybe that was a good thing. Finally, Mihi was learning how to act. Her whole life, she'd felt lost in a sea of Genevieves, who all somehow knew their way around. But now she'd discovered the guidebook: Sit up straight. But not too straight. Speak up. But not too loudly. Giggle, but don't snort. Let other people talk first. Smile.

And when it got hard to remember all those things at once, Mihi reminded herself: Every princess had challenges on their way to happily ever after. Following rules was just Mihi's challenge. And once she learned how to do that—*bam! Happiness!*

The biggest downside to her days was that they were so packed that she couldn't see Reese and Savannah. All she could think of was the looks on their faces when Mihi agreed to training, and she didn't know how they were feeling. Did they understand where she was coming from? Were they excited about the possibilities too? Or were they just getting angrier with her?

And then there were the nights. While Mihi lay in her too-big bed, fear and loneliness buzzed in her ears like a horde of homesick hornets. She missed the warmth of her mother's calloused fingertips running through her hair. She missed the way her father snort-laughed whenever she or her brother did something silly. She missed the way her grandmother winked at her whenever Mihi was feeling forgotten.

But all this would be worth it. Soon, the girls would *matter*.

On the third day, Bertha woke Mihi at the crack of dawn.

"One of our chefs will oversee your training today," she explained as she led Mihi through the twisting maze of castle halls. "I have other business to attend to."

When Bertha dropped Mihi off at the kitchen doors, Mihi tried not to cheer. As glad as she was not to train under Bertha's disapproving glare, she didn't want to be rude. Rudeness was probably unprincess-like.

After Bertha left, Mihi stepped into the kitchen, where she found an entire room made of gold. The countertops, the stove, the refrigerator—all of it glittered.

A cluster of cooks darted back and forth, filling the air with the frantic sounds of frying and chopping and dicing, all according to the orders of a short, round, red-faced man. He looked like a tomato with a mustache, and based on his extra tall hat, Mihi guessed he was the head chef.

The whole thing looked like the cooking shows Mihi watched with her mom—except for the fact that ingredients flew through the air all on their own. Cloves of garlic zipped through the room, their pungent scent trailing behind them. Carrots shimmied across countertops and hopped into a stew. An onion floated past Mihi, making her eyes water.

"*Magic,*" Mihi whispered. In her few days here, she'd seen magic all around her, and it made her giddy every time. But as Bertha had explained, not everybody is born with magic, and since Mihi wasn't, she'd just have to make do with being near it.

One of the cooks, probably just a few years older than Mihi, looked up and wiped sweat from her brow. "Ah, hello, you're early." Her tone was friendly enough, but she wouldn't quite meet Mihi's eyes. "We'll get started in just a moment. I'm Della, by the way."

"Hi, Della," Mihi said. "Are we doing a cooking lesson?" Memories of sizzling kalbi beef and steaming mandoo dumplings simmered in Mihi's thoughts, along with the now familiar taste of homesickness. Her stomach growled.

Della blinked in surprise. "Of course not. Princesses don't cook."

"Oh." It was all Mihi could say. The list of things princesses didn't do was growing at an alarming rate.

But before Della could tell Mihi what princesses *did* do, the cook rushed off to tend to her workstation.

Hoping to make herself useful, Mihi wandered over to the head chef and peeked at what he was making. Pasta with vegetables—which looked very nice, but was missing the savory scents of the noodles she'd grown up with.

"My parents make something like that, called japchae," Mihi told the chef, remembering her princess training. *Be gentle. Be calm. Be helpful.* She inched closer and closer, until she was standing by his elbow.

He looked at her, startled and displeased, and Mihi hesitated. Maybe he didn't understand that she was trying to be helpful.

"They use a lot of shoyu and sesame oil," she told him, "and stir it all together in a wok."

The chef grunted like he wanted Mihi to go away, but curiosity got the better of him. "What's a wok?"

Mihi tilted her head. "It's like a frying pan but bigger, and shaped kind of like a bowl."

The chef frowned, and Mihi expected him to tell her to go away. Instead, he said, "Interesting. I'll ask the blacksmith to make me one."

As the chef reached for a pad of paper and asked Mihi for a list of ingredients, she couldn't keep the smile from her face. She'd made a suggestion, a helpful suggestion, and the chef was going to listen. She was bringing stir-fry to Sleeping Beauty's castle! The thought was almost too thrilling to bear.

As if that wasn't exciting enough, the door swung open to reveal Reese and Savannah, who'd just been dropped off by their own ladies-in-waiting.

Without considering manners or etiquette or how princesses were supposed to behave, Mihi gasped and ran toward them, launching herself into a group hug. She hadn't realized just how worried she'd been.

Her friends hesitated for a moment, and Mihi pulled back a little. They were mad. She knew they'd be mad. But then Savannah gave her a squeeze.

"I didn't get a chance to explain," Mihi said. "I know Bertha said only one of us can win, but that can't be true, right? I was thinking maybe we could tie or something, and then we could all be princesses together."

Reese frowned a bit, but Savannah nodded. "I

knew it! I told Reese you'd never abandon us, even for something like this. That's brilliant, Mihi."

Mihi felt her shoulders relax. "Thank goodness we finally get to train together."

Reese leaned forward, her earlier hesitation seemingly forgotten. "I've been gathering information. We can compare notes."

Mihi grinned at them, but couldn't resist a glance at their princess pins. Mihi saw that they both had twenty-five points now. Mihi only had fifteen. Worry flickered in her heart. A tie seemed like a good idea, but she wasn't sure how to make that happen. She tried not to think about that as Della walked over to them.

"Oh, good," Della said. "We're all here, so we're ready to start the lesson."

Mihi noticed that Della's hands were shaking, but when the cook saw Mihi looking, she laced her fingers together. "We're going to decorate cakes."

Mihi's heart perked up. Though she'd hoped for a cooking lesson, decorating cakes could be fun too. At least, anything would be better than fainting.

"It's a tradition for the princess to decorate a cake before every ball," Della explained.

At this, Mihi's heart danced.

"A ball!" Savannah whispered into Mihi's ear.

Even Reese looked excited.

Della hesitated, noting the girls' reactions. "Um, I should let you know, though, that you're not, well, allowed to attend."

All the joy slid right out from under Mihi. But the worst part was seeing the expressions on Reese's and Savannah's faces. They'd been smiling, really smiling. And now . . .

"But! This isn't *just* cake decorating," Della added. "Because today, you'll be using magic."

ℰ Chapter 10 ℯ

"**O**r more accurately," Della continued, "you'll be using magic *dust.*"

"Dust?" Reese chewed her lip as if she were taking mental notes. Mihi could practically see her yearning for a pencil and paper.

Della pulled three velvet pouches from her apron— one blue, one green, and one red.

"Well, not *technically* dust," Della said. "More like ground-up pieces of magic. But dust is easier to say."

As Mihi reached for the red pouch, her hand brushed against Della's and the chef pulled back as if she'd been burned. "Sorry," she explained, as a blush heated her cheeks. "I'm not really used to . . . Greys."

So that was why Della was acting so strange, Mihi realized. She was *afraid* of them. The revelation was as sharp and painful as a bee sting. The mice had mentioned that some people didn't like Greys, but how could this nice girl be afraid of them? She didn't even know them.

Della cleared her throat to continue the training, and Mihi pushed her worries aside. There were more exciting things to focus on. "I'm sure your ladies-in-waiting have explained that not every role in every story has magic. But we've created a kind of cheat for when us non-magical folk really need it. We use the dust to perform tiny bouts of magic. Of course, the dust takes a long time to master, and it's no match for the real thing."

"This helps *us* do magic?" Savannah asked, awed.

"*This* helps us do magic?" Reese asked, doubtful.

"This helps us do *magic*." Mihi grinned.

"Again, very small bits of magic. But yes." Della opened the golden refrigerator (all three girls leaned over to check, but this fridge only had food inside—no portal to Medford), and pulled out three white cakes. From a drawer, she grabbed tubes of icing.

"The task itself is simple," she said. "Think of it like painting."

"I love painting," Reese said.

"Really?" Mihi asked. Reese seemed so focused on facts and numbers. And painting seemed so . . . not that.

Reese raised a brow. "Levitating food is not surprising to you, but me liking more than one thing is?"

For a moment, Mihi worried she'd offended Reese. But when Reese spoke, there was a hint of fondness in her words. "Your brain is wild, Mihi."

Mihi grinned. "That might be true."

Even Della smiled a bit at the exchange, and this time she actually made eye contact. "Now, pour a pinch of dust into your hand and rub your palms together. Focus on a tube of icing and find an emotional connection. It helps to think of a good memory involving icing. Then, flick your fingers as if you're controlling it. There's an art to this, so don't expect to be perfect on your first try."

Mihi untied her pouch, and when she tipped the dust into her hand, it prickled against her skin, as if she'd poured a porcupine into her palm.

"Fascinating," Reese murmured, squinting at her own handful.

"You're lucky," Della said, as the girls rubbed the dust between their palms. "Not many people would let Greys do this, but Bertha insisted that you learn."

Mihi, Reese, and Savannah exchanged a surprised glance. Mihi hadn't considered them lucky as far as Bertha was concerned, but the lady-in-waiting must really take their training seriously if she was willing to let them learn this.

"Are we sure this is safe?" Savannah whispered into Mihi's ear. "I don't trust Bertha."

Mihi frowned. Savannah had a point. But . . . "Cake decorating is harmless. And Della seems nice enough. She wouldn't do anything to hurt us."

Savannah frowned, but the temptation of magic was stronger than her fear. When they started practicing, she caught on first. She let out a startled yelp as the tube—directed by her fingers—lifted into the air and slowly moved toward the cake. Very carefully, she moved her fingers through the air, painting a perfect purple flower.

"Savannah!" Mihi cried. "You're amazing."

A grin spread across Savannah's face as she tried again. This time, she painted a perfect orange flower.

Reese figured it out next. "How is this possible?" she asked, as her own tube hovered above the table. But it was, and though she wasn't quite as skilled with the dust as Savannah, she learned fast. And she *was* great at painting. Before long, she'd created a scene of a beautiful blonde princess sitting on the grass. Sleeping Beauty.

Mihi still had nothing. She tried to think of a memory, but the only one that came to mind was Genevieve's birthday last year. As a gift, she'd wanted to sing a very special, totally unique song for her friend, instead of plain old "Happy Birthday," but Genevieve had sighed. *Not today, Mihi.*

As Mihi struggled, Reese leaned over and demonstrated the technique. Savannah murmured encouragements. Mihi pushed the bad memory away and tried to be positive. Icing was good. Who didn't like sugar?

Slowly but surely, warmth heated her palms, and her fingertips tingled with those porcupine prickles. As the icing began to vibrate on the table, Mihi felt the magic spreading up her arms and through her body, buzzing in her chest.

"I think I'm doing it," Mihi whispered.

"You are!" Savannah confirmed.

The grey icing lifted a millimeter into the air.

Mihi was so thrilled that she thought she might burst into triumphant song. But she needed to focus. The icing lifted a little higher, and the porcupine prickles traveled straight up into Mihi's nose—

And she sneezed.

A glob of grey icing flew far past her own cake and landed with a splat on Reese's.

Reese's eyes widened. Now, instead of a blonde princess, Reese's cake displayed a princess with a grey blob for hair. Even worse, when the icing hit the cake it pushed the whole design out of place, squishing the princess's smile into a grimace.

"Reese!" Mihi exclaimed, horrified. "I'm so, so sorry."

"She looks like . . ." Savannah whispered.

Eyes widening, Mihi finished, "She looks like *Bertha*."

Reese made a strangled noise, and Mihi's stomach sank. She'd completely ruined Reese's cake.

But then Reese burst out laughing. "Wild, Mihi," she said, once she'd caught her breath. "Totally wild."

Della cleared her throat in what sounded like a muffled laugh, and then backed away, as if to say, *I didn't see anything.*

"I can fix it!" Mihi promised.

But Savannah held up a hand. "Let me." With an impressive swish of her finger, she added big angry eyebrows to the icing-Bertha—and then all three girls were laughing.

This fairy-tale world, this castle, this prickly dust that let them lift tubes of icing into the air—it was all magical. But laughing with Reese and Savannah like this? That was a kind of magic too.

And then the door swung open. The kitchen filled with the sharp scent of toothpaste. A shadow fell over them.

Their laughter evaporated as they turned to see Bertha, surveying their work—Savannah's perfect cake, filled with cream flowers, Mihi's still-blank cake, and then . . . Reese's cake.

Mihi watched as Bertha realized what was on the cake. Her sour expression curdled.

Della and the head chef looked down, focusing

hard on their own cooking, avoiding Bertha's frosty glare.

"It's my fault," Mihi said quickly. "Don't blame Reese."

"I see," Bertha said. Her eyes caught the pad of paper near the chef station, and she stepped over to read it, narrowing her eyes at the recipe. "And I am assuming *this* is your doing too?"

The chef cleared his throat and hustled away, busying himself by rearranging ingredients in the pantry.

"I thought Sleeping Beauty might like japchae," Mihi said.

Bertha's expression tightened. "What did I say about change? It has consequences."

"Well, it's not *really* a change. It's just noodles."

"This is about more than noodles," she sighed. "There are bigger forces at work than you realize— powerful forces that care a great deal about keeping the sameness of these stories intact. And for good reason. People of both the Grey and Rainbow Realms rely on familiar fairy tales for security and guidance. Without these stories, both worlds would crumble."

Savannah frowned and Reese made a little *hmm* noise, but didn't elaborate. Mihi was used to getting in trouble, so she just nodded. But inside, something started to whir. She couldn't decide what she thought about Bertha's words.

On the one hand, she doubted japchae would crumble multiple worlds. But on the other hand, maybe Bertha was right—because what would Mihi's world be without these fairy tales? The stories were a bright spot. They were joy. They showed her who she wanted to be. Who she was *supposed* to be.

Bertha flicked her wrist, and Mihi felt something grow hot against her chest. She looked down to see a new number forming on her pin. When she glanced at Reese and Savannah, she saw theirs changing too. Now Reese had twenty-six points. Savannah had thirty. Mihi looked back at her own pin.

Her new total: ten. While Reese and Savannah had both earned points, Mihi had lost some. Now a tie seemed impossible.

Reese and Savannah looked at Mihi with dread in their eyes, and Mihi could tell they were all thinking the same thing.

For the first time since they'd arrived, Mihi truly understood: They wouldn't all become princesses. Only one of them would get her own happily ever after. And right now, Mihi was in last place.

She couldn't achieve her dreams and keep her friends at the same time.

All at once, Mihi realized that her biggest, greatest dream might come at a cost.

Chapter 11

By her fourth day, Mihi had graduated to tea party training—which should have been nice, considering it meant memorizing different kinds of tea and eating mini cakes all day.

But she was finding it hard to focus considering:

- Her gorgeous pink gown was squishing her internal organs to mush.
- She didn't want to be friendless.

Thinking about the competition had kept Mihi up all night. She still wanted to be a princess—so very badly—but the dream didn't have the same appeal when she was competing against her friends.

"You aren't focusing," Bertha sighed, annoyed as

usual. "If you don't pay attention to tea tasting, you'll never be a princess. Not that it matters to *me*."

Mihi still wasn't sure what tea tasting had to do with being a princess, so she decided to take a risk. Bertha hated questions, but Mihi had *so many*. "Can't my friends and I be princesses together?"

Bertha's jaw twitched. "No."

"But we could be part of the same story! We could rule a kingdom together."

"No."

"But queens and kings rule kingdoms together. So what's the difference if a group of friends did?"

Bertha's gaze was cold. "There is no *ruling kingdoms* here. The stories are already written, and people live by them."

Mihi frowned. "But what happens when . . . problems come up? Shouldn't someone try to fix them?"

"In a happily ever after, there *are* no problems."

"Oh. Right." Mihi tried to picture it. A world without problems. No pet chaos. No trips to the principal's office. No Genevieves. No wondering if she'd ever fit in anywhere. "I guess that does sound nice."

A flicker of emotion passed over Bertha's face. Sadness, maybe. No. Even more than that. *Sorrow*.

But then Bertha cleared her throat and her expression settled back to stone. Again, Mihi thought she'd imagined it.

"It's time for our weekly castle-wide nap. We do this to practice." Bertha glanced at her watch. "And, of course, to rest for the ball tonight."

Mihi sat a little straighter. "The ball!"

"Let me be clear: Princesses in training do *not* attend balls."

Mihi chewed her lip. Whoever succeeded in training would be allowed to attend balls, and the other two wouldn't. But . . . Mihi remembered how excited her friends had looked when they'd heard about the ball. They *had* to go. This was a chance for *all* of them to be the princess type—no matter who won the competition.

Bertha stood. "When I return from my nap in an hour, I expect you to know each tea by heart. Then we will clean the castle."

An hour of tea tasting? Followed by cleaning? And *no ball*?

As Bertha left the room, Mihi felt that itch-itch-itch growing inside her. She had to *do* something. And now she had a whole hour free from Bertha.

Mihi stuffed cakes into her dress pockets, alongside pieces of lint and the rolled-up candy-wrapper map. Then she tiptoed out of the dining room. Mihi had a plan, and if all went well, she and her friends would go to this ball.

Because Bertha had a lot of power in the castle—but Mihi knew there was someone with even more, someone who could overrule the head lady-in-waiting.

Mihi was about to break the first rule of training.

She was going to meet the princess.

Chapter 12

Mihi hurried into the grand ballroom and up the golden staircase, feeling grateful for the castle-wide nap hour. Nobody was around. This was her window of opportunity.

When she reached the top of the staircase, Mihi held her hand in front of Sleeping Beauty's door, ready to knock—but her stomach twisted. What if this was a bad idea? What if Sleeping Beauty told Bertha that Mihi had broken a rule, and Bertha kicked Mihi out of training?

On the other hand, this was Mihi's one chance to get her and her friends to the ball. And how could Mihi sit in this castle, in this fairy-tale land, in this one-in-a-million, once-in-a-lifetime, once-in-a-*million*-lifetimes opportunity, and *not* meet Sleeping Beauty?

She knocked hard. Her heart slammed against her chest.

And . . . nothing happened.

Mihi knocked again.

When the door stayed shut, Mihi realized . . . this was the *castle-wide* nap hour. Sleeping Beauty must be *sleeping*. Obviously.

Her cheeks burned. How could she have missed something so evident?

But as she turned away, the door cracked open, and a single blue eye peered out.

"Hello?" The princess's voice was as warm and sweet as gold-spun honey.

"Hi!" Mihi said, too loudly. *Be calm, Mihi.* She cleared her throat and spoke at a normal volume. "Hi, I came to ask you something. Which is really cool. Because you're Sleeping Beauty."

The door cracked open a bit more to reveal a girl about Mihi's age, with big eyes, a button nose, and soft blonde curls tied back with a ribbon. "I'm sorry. I don't believe we've met."

"Oh, right. I'm Mihi. I'm . . . new here." Mihi

tried to smile like she wasn't freaking out, like she wasn't meeting a *fairy-tale princess*. She worried she might actually faint, but on the bright side, she'd get to put all that practice to use.

The princess smiled. "We don't get a lot of new people around here. Where are you from?"

"I'm from—" Mihi paused. Based on what the mice had said and on Della's reaction to their arrival, people from her world were rare—and maybe not very well-liked. She didn't know how Sleeping Beauty would take it. "I'm from the forest." That seemed good enough. She *had* been in the forest. Maybe the princess would think she was from the treehouse village? Surely lots of people lived there?

Sleeping Beauty opened the door wider, eyes bright with interest. "And how'd you end up here?"

"I'm here because . . . I'm a princess too." Oh no. The words had just popped out. How horrifying. Sleeping Beauty would sense the lie immediately. She'd see that Mihi wasn't the princess type.

But Sleeping Beauty threw the door open. "Oh thank *goodness*. So you understand!" She grabbed

Mihi's hand, dragging her inside and pushing the door shut behind her. "I've wanted someone to talk to for *so long*. Are you one of those new princesses? You are all so *cool*."

Mihi stumbled after Sleeping Beauty. Stepping into her bedroom was like walking into a cloud. Everything was soft and white and fluffy. It smelled like clean sheets and rain.

But it was also . . . kind of boring. Peaceful and relaxing, sure, but there wasn't anything to *do*. No books or games or anything.

Sleeping Beauty spoke quickly. "How are you? How was your day? What is the *forest* like?"

Mihi blinked. She hadn't expected the princess to be so . . . enthusiastic. Enthusiasm wasn't a part of princess training. And this was quite a lot of questions considering the most important rule of being a princess was: *No asking questions.*

"Um. I'm good! My day was good! And the forest is colorful."

"Colorful," the princess said, like she was tasting the word. "Like gold?"

"No. Not like gold. Like a rainbow?"

"You know, I've never met someone from the forest before. I've never even been outside the castle grounds. Is that weird? I never considered it, but now that I've met you, I think that might be weird!"

In truth, it did strike Mihi as a little strange. If she were the princess, living in this magical world, she'd want to see *everything*. But then again, what did Mihi know? She wasn't a princess. She was just . . . herself.

"So, tell me," Sleeping Beauty said, eyes lit up, "what's it like living in the forest?"

Mihi, of course, had no idea how to answer that. "Oh, you know," she said, though neither of them did. "How was *your* day?"

If Sleeping Beauty noticed the abrupt change of subject, she didn't say anything. She flopped onto her bed, and a puff of white mist floated up around her. Mihi peered closer. Was her bed made of *actual clouds?*

"I have nothing to complain about." Sleeping Beauty leaned forward, resting her elbows on her knees. "But of course, everything is always the same, every day. I sing to animals in the morning, though they don't usually listen—have you noticed? They can be so rude. Then I try to sleep during nap hour, but I never can. Then I practice fainting. Oh, I've gotten pretty good at that, would you like to see?"

Mihi blinked. "Oh, no, no thanks."

"Are you sure? The trick is to have a code word. Mine is sugarplums. Anytime someone says 'sugarplums' I immediately drop to the floor. Though I haven't quite figured out the sleeping part of it yet."

"Well, that's still impressive."

Sleeping Beauty beamed. But after a moment, her smile wobbled, and her face fell.

Mihi could have sworn she recognized that expression. She could have sworn she'd felt that exact way—like her life was not the life she wanted. Like she was meant for something bigger, but was trapped in clothes two sizes too small.

But that didn't make sense. Sleeping Beauty was a *princess*. "Is everything okay?" Mihi asked.

Sleeping Beauty sighed. "Sometimes I feel like I'm sleepwalking through my own life."

Mihi frowned. "If you feel that way, why don't you change it?"

The princess tilted her head. "Change my life? But how?"

Mihi didn't know what to say. Bertha's warning echoed in her head, but Mihi wasn't talking about *big, bad* changes. Just good little ones, like eating something new for dinner, or going outside every once in a while. "I—"

Sleeping Beauty's stomach growled, loudly interrupting Mihi's train of thought. "Sorry, I get so hungry during nap hour and I always have to wait for everyone to wake up."

"Oh!" Mihi said, remembering. "I have tea cakes." She dug them out of her pockets. They were covered in fuzz, but they'd still taste good. She blew the lint off.

"Thank you so very much!" Sleeping Beauty took the treats, holding them up to the light and marveling. "You are the nicest person in the world."

The princess stuffed a cake into her mouth, looking like she might cry tears of joy. Mouth full, she said, "I get all my meals delivered in that dumbwaiter over there." She pointed to what looked like a small elevator. "It's like an elevator for food. Well, more like feasts. The chefs can get elaborate."

Mihi inspected the dumbwaiter. It was much smaller than a regular elevator, but not *that* small. Mihi guessed it would fit three of her, if she squished. She wondered if Sleeping Beauty would now get perfect bowls of japchae delivered right to her bedroom.

"It's all delicious, don't get me wrong," Sleeping Beauty continued. "But I don't get many desserts. And never *surprise* desserts! Thank you!"

"You're welcome." Mihi grinned, feeling a little giddy. She'd made Sleeping Beauty happy. *She* had— Mihi!

And then she remembered: She had a purpose here. "Hey, so remember how I said I was a princess?" She swallowed.

Sleeping Beauty nodded as she chewed a second tea cake.

"Well, ah, I'm actually a princess in *training*," Mihi forced the words out, embarrassment heating her cheeks, "with my friends. And Bertha is making us do all this boring stuff, but we were hoping to do fun things too. Like going to the ball tonight!"

Sleeping Beauty winced. "Oh, right. The ball. I hate those. I always feel like something bad's about to happen there. But if you want to go, just ask Bertha."

"Um, Bertha doesn't seem like the biggest fan of questions," Mihi said. "She made it pretty clear that we weren't invited. And she's kinda scary."

Sleeping Beauty waved off the concern. "Bertha's not as scary as she seems. Tell her I said it's okay, and she'll do it."

"Really? Just like that?"

"Of course! Easy."

Nothing with Bertha seemed easy, but maybe with the princess's approval, everything would be different. "That's great," Mihi said. "Thank you."

She glanced at the clock on Sleeping Beauty's wall. Nap hour was almost over. Mihi had gotten what she wanted—she'd met a fairy-tale princess *and* gotten permission to do something amazingly fun with her friends. They could worry about the competition *after*. Now it was time to go, before Bertha caught her.

But seeing the princess like this tugged at Mihi's chest. Being a princess was all Mihi had ever wanted, but Sleeping Beauty didn't have a choice. She was like the birds in her parents' animal shelter. Beautiful, but trapped.

"Um, just a random thought . . ." Mihi said slowly. "Uh, how would you feel about, I don't know, pricking your finger on a spinning wheel and falling asleep for a hundred years until a prince kissed you awake?"

The princess wrinkled her nose. "Huh?"

Mihi forced a laugh. "Just a super random question that popped into my head. I'm doing a . . . poll of everyone I talk to." Sure, Bertha had specifically told Mihi not to mention the story to the princess, but this was different. This was a *hypothetical*. So it was fine.

"That's very odd," Sleeping Beauty said. "But I would hate that. I hate nap hour, and I'm not interested in any prince."

"Oh, okay. Good to know." Mihi skimmed her memory, trying to recall everything she knew about

Sleeping Beauty's fairy tale. If the princess didn't know about the spinning wheel, but she still lived in the castle, this must be like the Brothers Grimm version of the tale. Sleeping Beauty had no idea that a fairy had enchanted her as a baby, that she'd prick her finger and fall into a century-long sleep.

So now what?

Mihi cleared her throat. "Um, another super random thought. Maybe you should wear gloves. Like, all the time."

Sleeping Beauty's brows pinched. She looked a little like Reese when she was trying to figure something out.

"You are a very strange person," the princess said finally. "But I like you."

"Ha ha, yeah." Mihi remembered, too late, how disastrous it had been when she'd tried to set the birds free.

But how could she let Sleeping Beauty walk into a trap—especially knowing how much she'd hate her fate? "Gloves, I'm telling you. They're very trendy now. I promise."

Sleeping Beauty shrugged. "If you say so . . ."

"Okay, great. Gloves!" Mihi blurted out, glancing over at the clock. She only had a few minutes. "I have to go now. It was nice to meet you! Bye!"

Then she bolted out the door—and ran straight into someone.

For a sickening moment she thought it was Bertha, but it wasn't Bertha at all.

It was Savannah.

And she looked terrified.

Chapter 13

Like Mihi, Savannah wore a ball gown—this one blue and poufy and not at all Savannah's style. Her face was pale, and her eyes wide. "We have to go," she blurted, grabbing Mihi's sleeve and dragging her down the stairs.

"Whoa." Mihi scrambled to keep her balance. "What's going on?"

"The horse. It's out to get me."

Mihi paused. "The . . . horse?"

Savannah didn't stop. As they ran down the staircase, she said, "That was my task today. To tend to the stables and bond with the horses. But there's *one* horse in particular. She hates me."

"Savannah, it's a *horse*. It doesn't hate you."

"I can tell by the way it sniffs me. I'm serious, Mihi.

Horses are dangerous. They can bite and stomp and toss you to your doom."

When they reached the bottom of the staircase, Mihi gripped Savannah's hands and squeezed. "Savannah, don't worry. The horses won't hurt you. We're in a *fairy tale*."

"And fairy tales are dangerous, remember? I just keep thinking about all the stories I've heard, and waiting for something scary to pop out. I don't think I'm cut out for this."

Mihi glanced at Savannah's pin. With thirty-five points, she was still way ahead of Mihi. And though Mihi was supposed to be competing with Savannah, the idea of her giving up now was so sad. "But, Savannah, we're safe here. And you're doing so well—you have so many points. Don't you want to stay?"

Savannah bit her lip. "Mihi, all this training just isn't what I imagined."

"Just stay a little longer," Mihi pleaded, though the tiniest part of her maybe-sort-of agreed with Savannah. "I found a way to go to the ball."

Savannah hesitated. "Really?"

The front doors banged open, and Reese ran in. "There you are! We have to get out of here."

Mihi's heart sank. Not Reese too.

Savannah frowned. "Reese, it's like they . . . tried to make you look like Princess Tiana."

Reese wore a poufy green dress, and her hair, which she always wore loose and curly, was pulled into a tight bun on top of her head, secured with a boatload of hair gel and bobby pins.

Reese rolled her eyes. "I had 'makeover training' this morning."

Mihi frowned. "Can you take it out? It looks painful."

Reese held her hands up. "It is, but that's not my main concern. The bigger problem is I can't figure this place out."

"It's magic," Mihi said.

Reese nodded. "Exactly."

Mihi and Savannah exchanged a glance.

"So," Savannah said carefully, "after talking mice, magic dust, and storybook castles, you finally admit we're in a magical fairy-tale world?"

Reese glanced around and lowered her voice. Mihi and Savannah leaned in. In their shiny ball gowns, the three of them looked very much like princesses. Scheming princesses.

"Yesterday, after the magic dust thing, I changed my official hypothesis to 'yes, this is in fact magic,'" Reese said. "And I spent all night going over that theory. At this point, it's the only thing that makes sense."

"But magic is a *good* thing," Mihi insisted.

"Sure, when it's castles and cakes," Reese said. "But magic also means there's no logical explanation. And if we can't explain this world, how do we know how to live in it?"

"But maybe it's okay if we can't explain everything," Mihi protested. "Maybe we can figure it out as we go, and be surprised and excited. That's an adventure."

Reese shook her head. "Look, during the nap hour, my lady-in-waiting sent me outside to 'smell the roses.' Which was boring. But I found these black, thorny weeds, so I thought I'd be helpful. I plucked a weed, and just seconds later, it grew back taller than before. That's an evil curse, for sure."

"Oh no," Savannah whispered.

Mihi's breath hitched. "Thorny vines in Sleeping Beauty's tale aren't . . . great."

Reese nodded. "Fairy tales aren't all roses. They're full of thorns too. And I don't think we're safe here."

"I don't either," Savannah said, and Mihi's heart fell. "Even though I really want to go to that ball."

"Fairy tales can be dangerous," Mihi agreed reluctantly. The reward was worth the risk for Mihi, but maybe it wasn't for her friends. Still, she could do something good for them before they decided to leave. "But . . . we *do* know some things about this world. We know how Sleeping Beauty's story is supposed to go. And in the stories, Sleeping Beauty doesn't prick her finger during a ball, so we know the ball will be safe. I got us invited, so we can have fun together for a night. And then, if you still want to, you can leave before things go wrong."

"I suppose we *could* use that knowledge to our advantage," Reese said carefully. She tilted her head. "How'd you get us invited to the ball?"

Mihi explained meeting Sleeping Beauty.

"Everything will be okay now," she insisted, when she'd finished telling them about the princess and her white cloud bedroom.

Mihi didn't mention the other stuff, exactly—like how sad and lonely the princess seemed. Or how Mihi had felt a wave of nausea when she thought of the princess's future . . . Or how Mihi had told her to wear gloves . . .

Reese nodded slowly. "And you're sure Bertha will agree?"

Savannah said, "Bertha's first rule was not to talk to Sleeping Beauty, and it seems like a bad idea to break Bertha's rules. But what can Bertha say if the princess already agreed?" And then she added, like she couldn't resist, "Was Sleeping Beauty cool?"

Mihi grinned. "She was so cool. And nice too."

Reese swallowed. "Do you think we could meet her too? If we go to the ball?"

"Of course! She'd be so happy!"

Mihi looked at her friends and saw, beneath their fear and worry, that still-burning hope.

Savannah bit her lip. "Okay, let's do it."

Mihi inhaled as deeply as her dress would let her, trying to hold in her giddy excitement. "That's great. Now all we have to do is tell Bertha."

Behind them, they heard the clack-clack of heels, and the scent of toothpaste wafted into the room. The lady-in-waiting's voice was cold as ice. "Tell me what?"

Chapter 14

"Oh, hi, Bertha!" Mihi put on her best *look how obedient and not-sneaky I am!* smile. "We were just about to come see you!"

Bertha raised a thin brow. "None of you are where you should be."

Mihi cleared her throat. "Uh, that is correct. But it's because we have something very important to talk to you about."

Her friends nodded, following her lead.

Bertha sighed. "Very well. Come to my office."

The girls followed Bertha through the castle, through winding corridors they hadn't explored before, up and down staircases, and finally, into a large office that smelled like worn paper.

Bertha took a seat at her desk and gestured to three chairs across from her.

Mihi sat, feeling like she was in her principal's office, waiting to be sent to indoor recess.

"What is it?" Bertha demanded.

Savannah shrank in her seat. Reese's eyes went wide behind her red frames. And Mihi took a deep breath. If Bertha didn't want her asking questions, she'd make a statement instead. "We're going to the ball."

For a moment, Bertha sat in shock. Then her eyes narrowed. "And what, exactly, makes you think you're ready for that?"

"We've been training hard for a few days now," Mihi began. "And—and I talked to Sleeping Beauty—"

"You *what?*" Bertha's voice sharpened.

"I know, and I'm sorry, but she said we're ready—"

Bertha scoffed. "She doesn't know what she's talking about."

"But . . . she's the princess."

"Exactly."

Mihi glanced at her friends, but they looked just as confused as she did.

"What does a *princess* know about the world?" Bertha continued.

Sleeping Beauty's words echoed in Mihi's head. *I've never even been outside the castle grounds.*

Reese frowned. "Isn't that the whole point of training?"

Bertha pursed her lips. "You can train as much as you like, but a princess doesn't get to decide when she's ready. The job of a princess is to wait. You wait for your story to begin."

Mihi's throat tightened. "We have to wait?"

"Of course. Wait for your prince to come, wait for your fate to unravel, wait for an evil curse to get things started."

Savannah said, very softly, "And what do we do while we wait?"

Bertha waved a hand. "Paint and faint. Garden. Learn to knit. Have you ever heard of Sudoku? Those puzzles are enchanting."

Bertha did not sound enchanted.

"You don't get a say in your future," Bertha continued. "That's what you signed up for. And you should be grateful you're even getting this training."

"We are, but . . ." Mihi swallowed. She hated

when adults accused her of being ungrateful. She always tried to be appreciative, but sometimes opportunities didn't feel entirely good, or right.

"Unless you don't actually want to become a princess." For a moment, Bertha looked curious rather than disdainful.

This was their chance to leave, to go home, to see their families. Her friends were right, things might get dangerous. But princesses weren't supposed to give up. They always worked through trials and difficulties, because in the end they got a happy, wonderful life, in a world where they belonged. "I still want to," Mihi murmured.

Bertha glanced at her watch. "Well, shoo," she said, as if she hadn't heard Mihi at all. "I have a meeting to attend."

Bertha stood, waving her arms at them like she was trying to get rid of a rotten smell. As soon as the girls stood, Bertha pushed them out of her office.

Then she slammed the door.

Mihi, Reese, and Savannah stared at each other, stunned.

"Mihi . . ." Reese said finally. "I'm gonna ask Bertha to send me home."

Savannah nodded. "Me too. But I guess this is good? You won't have any competition. Your dream will come true."

Savannah was right. So why didn't Mihi feel happy? Why did she have that fluttering feeling that something was wrong? She forced a smile. "And we can still hang out at school, right? When I'm back?" She tried to sound cheerful, but the words came out heavy.

"Of course," Savannah said.

Reese held up her fist to knock, but just as she was about to pound on Bertha's door, Savannah grabbed her wrist.

"Wait," she whispered, leaning forward to press her ear against the door. "Do you hear that?"

Mihi and Reese listened through the wood. Bertha was speaking louder than usual, so her words seeped through the thick mahogany.

"You're early." Bertha sounded annoyed, which is to say Bertha sounded like she always did. "You know I hate it when you teleport like that. It's quite unsettling."

Bertha paused, and Mihi heard someone else speaking, though she couldn't make out their response.

"I know you wanted to have some fun with the Greys," Bertha said. Now she sounded even more annoyed than usual. "But you know how the magic in our world reacts to change. The castle is already reacting to their presence. This morning, I noticed some vines—"

The other speaker interrupted, and all three girls strained to make out their words—but they couldn't quite hear.

Bertha responded, "Yes, I know we can't actually send them home."

Mihi's heart stuttered. She looked at her friends, eyes wide.

The muffled response again, and then Bertha sighed. "Yes, Houdini, I am aware. They must be disposed of."

At that, Mihi's heart stopped completely.

Houdini?? Savannah mouthed.

Disposed of??? Reese mouthed back.

Mihi couldn't believe they had trusted that mouse.

Through the door, Bertha said, "Don't worry about it. I'll handle them, right after I finish this Sudoku."

Mihi stumbled away from the door, heartbeat roaring in her ears.

"What do we do?" Savannah whispered.

"We need to get out of here as fast as possible," Reese spoke quickly. "On some magical thing, like a dragon, or a flying bicycle, or—"

Mihi turned to Savannah. "A horse."

Savannah's eyes flashed with panic, and Mihi leaned forward. "Sav, I know it's scary. But our options are that horse, or *disposal*."

"Okay," Savannah said, squaring her shoulders. "Follow me. *Run*."

Chapter 15

Mihi and her friends sprinted through the castle. Ladies-in-waiting, servants, and cooks all watched in confusion as the girls scrambled past.

"Disposed of!" Mihi gasped as they ran. "That's the most evil phrase I've ever heard."

"You said you wanted adventure," Reese gasped back.

"Not in a *murder-y* way!"

"How do you think she'll dispose of us?" Savannah asked as they ran through the grand ballroom. The intricate castle mural looked menacing now, with its bright colors and happy scene. Everything felt *wrong*.

"Probably best not to think about that," Reese replied.

The girls threw the front doors open and tumbled

out, clutching at their sides as they ran toward the stables.

They were halfway there when Savannah shrieked. Stumbling, Reese and Mihi turned to see her sprawled on the ground. A thorny, black vine was wrapped around her ankle.

"The weeds!" Reese cried.

Savannah tugged herself free, losing one of her shoes in the process. "What was that?" she gasped.

As she got to her feet, another weed broke the surface, just in front of Reese. Reese dodged, and the girls ran even faster as the vines burst up around them.

Mihi yelped. "You were right about the weeds, Reese!"

"Normally, I love to hear those words," Reese panted. "But right now, I really, really wish I'd been wrong."

They sprinted, weaving between the weeds, and they'd nearly reached the stables when one of those vines sprang up and wrapped around Mihi's calf.

She tugged, but it only wrapped tighter. Another vine coiled around her waist.

Pain and panic clouded Mihi's vision. She squirmed helplessly against the vine, but as it squeezed her chest, she began to feel light-headed. Distantly, she wondered if these were the consequences Bertha had mentioned—if by changing the dinner menu and visiting Sleeping Beauty, Mihi really had disrupted too much.

Reese and Savannah screamed, and Mihi knew they were trapped too. Mihi squirmed, punching the vine, but it was useless. The vine barely reacted to her blows.

"We need something sharp to cut these away," she gasped.

But of course, they didn't have anything. The only thing Mihi had in her pockets was the map. She had nothing at all, except . . .

"The pin!" she shouted, as she ripped the princess pin off her dress. The pin's needle was a tiny weapon.

She plunged it into the vine.

Black sludge burst out, oozing over Mihi, and the vine recoiled, releasing her. She scrambled to her feet.

Her friends followed suit, and before the vines could grab them again, they sprinted.

Savannah threw the stable doors open and led Reese and Mihi to a white mare with a black star on her forehead.

"Hi, Starr, I know you're not my biggest fan, but this is life or death," Savannah panted desperately. "So will you please help us flee, and not bite or stomp or throw us off?"

The horse snorted as a vine exploded up through the stable floor, and Savannah yelped, "I'm gonna take that as a yes!"

Grabbing Starr's mane, she pulled herself up, then offered a hand to help her friends. Once they'd all scrambled on, Savannah kicked the horse's sides, and Starr reared.

Mihi wrapped her arms around Reese, who wrapped her arms around Savannah, who wrapped her arms around the horse's neck, and it was all they could do to keep from falling—and then Starr took off, jostling the girls as she galloped out of the stables, darting past the vines.

Mihi called out, "This is horrifying!"

But when Savannah turned, her brown hair whipping around her, she looked regal. She looked strong. She looked . . . brave. "It is," she said, with wonder in her voice, "but it's also kind of exciting."

Mihi barely recognized this confidence in Savannah, and despite nearly being disposed of by Bertha and strangled by vines, she began to feel a little better.

As they galloped away from the castle, Mihi told herself that everything was going to be okay.

Chapter 16

Starr carried them through the forest, weaving between trees. Every once in a while, they brushed so close to the branches that leaves snagged in Mihi's hair, and she held her breath, trying not to panic.

From the front of the horse, Savannah shouted into the whistling wind, "Where are we going?"

"For now? Just away!" Reese responded. "Mihi, do you still have the map?"

Holding tight to Reese with one hand, Mihi stuck the other into her pocket, reaching for the map. As her fingers brushed against the paper, she felt something else—something smooth and cold.

Frowning, Mihi handed the map to Reese before reaching back in and pulling out the mysterious object.

It was heavy and circular, the size of her palm, and

it was made of tarnished silver. Carved into the metal was a heart with a rose in the center. This looked like something Mihi could have found at a flea market. Etched on the back in small letters were the words: *Made in Stonington.*

Without taking her eyes off the object, Mihi asked, "Do you guys know where Stonington is?"

Reese attempted to read the map while bouncing up and down. "I don't see it on here."

"It's written on this . . . thing." On closer inspection, Mihi found a small button, and when she pressed it the object popped open like a locket. Inside was a compass with an arrow that spun and spun, refusing to stop.

Savannah turned to see. "Where'd that come from?"

"It was in my pocket, but I never put it there." Mihi frowned.

Reese shook her head, still inspecting the map. "Maybe one of the seamstresses left it in your pocket. Or maybe you picked it up and forgot about it."

Mihi thought back, but she could only recall that moment in Sleeping Beauty's bedroom when she'd reached into her pockets to pull out the cakes. Her pockets had been empty except for the map. She was certain of that.

Reese returned to the map. "We're headed in the direction of that tree village. Going back to the mice's tree is out, obviously. But there must be somewhere else to go." She leaned closer to the map, squinting at the labels.

But before Reese could decide, Starr spooked. The horse reared, and Savannah screamed, her knuckles whitening as she gripped Starr's mane. "Hold on!" she cried.

Mihi felt gravity shift beneath her, pulling her to the earth, but she resisted. She squeezed her eyes shut and wrapped her arms around Reese, hanging on as tightly as she possibly could.

It wasn't tight enough.

Chapter 17

It happened fast. One moment Mihi, Reese, and Savannah were slipping off the horse, and the next—a sharp burst of pain.

They hit the ground hard, and Starr became a speck of white as she galloped, riderless, into the forest.

Slowly, Mihi's pain began to fade, but it was immediately replaced with fear. Starr was their only way of escaping. Without the horse, Bertha would catch up quickly.

Reese didn't waste time on panic. With a deep breath and steely determination, she stood. Her dress was ripped and covered in dirt, but she seemed uninjured. "We need to put more distance between us and the castle. Bertha will realize we're gone soon—if she hasn't already—and we're much slower on foot."

Mihi pushed herself off the ground. Gently, she rolled out her wrists and rubbed an aching spot on her hip that she knew would bruise. She was sore, but other than that she was okay. "Agreed. Let's keep moving."

They turned to Savannah, but she was still crumpled on the ground.

"Sav?" Mihi murmured. She tasted fear, sharp and sour on her tongue.

Savannah groaned. "My *ankle*."

Mihi knelt beside her and pushed the hem of Savannah's dress up, revealing her bare foot. Her ankle was swollen and purple.

"Does it look bad to you?" Savannah asked.

Reese and Mihi exchanged a glance.

"Um . . ." Reese said.

"It doesn't look great?" Mihi tried.

Savannah squeezed her eyes shut, and Reese mouthed to Mihi, *Is it broken?*

I don't know, Mihi mouthed back.

"Well, we can't walk," Reese said. "So we need somewhere to hide."

Mihi glanced around. They were exposed, in the middle of a path, just waiting to be disposed of. But a few yards away, she spotted a cluster of rocks that formed a makeshift cave. "What about there?"

Reese nodded. "Good enough for now."

She and Mihi each ducked beneath one of Savannah's arms, and slowly but surely, they lifted her. Savannah put all her weight on her good foot and took a deep breath. "Okay," she said. "I've got this."

Savannah's face was a ghostly white and she swallowed hard with every step, but with Reese and Mihi's help, she managed to limp over to the cave.

Savannah's voice trembled as her friends set her down, safely tucked out of sight. "What do we do? What do we do?"

"We have to find a way home," Reese responded. "But we can't do that if you can't walk."

And then Mihi had an idea. "The Healing Orchard!"

Reese thought for a moment. "That might be a good option. But it's so close to the mice's tree. We could get caught. And we don't even know if any of that is *actually* healing, or if it's a horrible trick."

Savannah groaned in pain, and both Reese and Mihi winced.

"Then again," Reese said, "I'm not sure what other options we have."

"I can't walk there," Savannah murmured through the pain. "Please don't leave me."

Mihi and Reese locked eyes, a silent conversation passing between them. *Should they stay? Should they go? How could they keep each other safe?*

"You stay with Savannah," Mihi said. "I'll go."

Reese frowned. "It's dangerous to go off on your own."

Mihi squared her shoulders, pretending she was braver than she was, pretending her heart wasn't hiccupping and her stomach wasn't flipping and her ears weren't echoing with the words *dispose of, dispose of, dispose of.* "I'll be fine."

Savannah's eyes filled with tears, and she hesitated for a moment before saying, "Thank you."

Mihi smiled, and though she was afraid and uncertain, her smile was a real one. She took the map from Reese, checked the compass in her pocket, which still didn't seem to work, and then walked away from her friends and into the forest.

"Going to the orchard, going to the orchard," she whispered to herself, attempting to sound light and brave. "Just going to the orchard to get something for Savannah."

She tried to make a little song out of it, but that just creeped her out, so she stopped.

Then it was silent, and fear crawled up Mihi's spine. Around her, the colors of the forest were too bright. Too *harsh*. She missed the soft fall foliage of Medford, Massachusetts. She missed her brother listing off facts about all the different species and native plants.

Had Mihi made the biggest mistake of her life by agreeing to be here? Had Genevieve been right about Mihi all along? Maybe she'd been silly to believe she could be someone important. To believe she could matter.

Her fingers reached for her crown necklace, like they often did when she felt lost—but she came up empty. She'd forgotten. She'd traded it away to those terrible mice.

She fought the urge to cry. Her mom had given that necklace to her three birthdays ago. Park Pet Rescue had been struggling that year, even more than usual, so Mihi hadn't expected or asked for presents.

But that night, her mom had sat on Mihi's bed and handed her this necklace.

"We believe in you, Mihi," she'd said. "You can achieve any dream you want, as long as you work hard enough."

Mihi would get that necklace back. Eventually, one day, she would. But for now, she had to push on. She had to keep going. Reese and Savannah were depending on her.

The forest grew denser, and when Mihi began to worry about finding her way back, inspiration struck. With one fierce tug, she ripped the poufy sleeve from her dress, and then tore the fabric into thin strips. Reaching up, she tied a strip to a tree branch.

When she'd gone a little farther, she tied another and began to feel better.

A makeshift breadcrumb trail. She'd learned a thing or two from fairy tales after all.

She consulted the map again. Unfortunately, the

magic trail Houdini had lit up on their map had faded, and without a path to follow, Mihi had no sense of where she was or how to get to the Healing Orchard.

She pulled that mysterious compass back out of her pocket and opened it. It spun and spun like it had before—and then, to Mihi's surprise, it stopped.

Mihi had studied compasses in a science unit once, but this needle didn't move like it was supposed to. It didn't rock back and forth before landing on north.

Instead, this reminded Mihi of watching *Wheel of Fortune* with her grandfather. The wheel spun, around and around, until it slowed down, ticking closer and closer to the contestant's fate. Would they be lucky? It was entirely up to chance.

Now, the needle pointed in one direction without moving, and Mihi looked up into the forest.

"Please help me," she whispered to the compass. "And please don't turn out to be an evil object leading me straight into danger."

Mihi didn't have a good feeling about this. But she also didn't know what to do.

So she followed it.

Chapter 18

Mihi followed the needle for what felt like hours. Her feet hurt. Her heart hurt. Her whole body hurt.

And still, she had no idea where she was. She was just walking, one foot in front of the other, following a red needle in a silver compass in a rainbow wood.

After walking for so long with her eyes on the compass, she was shocked to look up and find herself face-to-face with a tree.

She had nearly walked straight into its trunk.

Right, Mihi, she told herself, *Watch where you're going.* Even the reprimand brought a bubble of warmth to her chest. How many times had her parents told her that, when she'd stubbed her toes on the furniture or knocked over boxes of dog food in the storeroom?

What wouldn't she give to hear them say those words now?

Mihi stepped around the trunk—but something strange happened. As soon as she passed it, the needle spun around, pointing back at the tree.

Mihi frowned at the compass, then at the tree. Embarrassment tingled in her cheeks. She'd been following this tiny needle the whole time, throwing all of her hopes into this rusted piece of metal, which had come from who knows where. And this whole time, it had been broken.

She'd been following a broken compass.

She felt the hot prick of tears and looked up, willing the rush of emotion away—and that's when she realized.

Right above her was the treehouse village. And the house perched on the apple tree in front of her was the same one Mihi had seen earlier—the one that had given her that jittery, unsettled feeling. The little twist in her chest that said *there's a story here.*

Maybe this was a coincidence. But Mihi knew coincidences were rare in fairy tales. Her earlier fear rose up: Maybe there *was* something evil about this compass. Maybe it had led her straight into danger.

But even if it had . . . there was a silver lining: They'd passed this village right before they saw the orchard. Which meant she knew exactly how to get there.

Mihi spun around, but just as she turned away from the tree she heard the creak of hinges far above her.

Looking up, she saw the bloodred door to the treehouse swing open, and she knew she should run, knew it down to her bones. *She should run.*

But her feet stayed rooted to the earth. Her eyes stayed pinned to that door.

She expected something terrifying—an evil witch, a mastermind mouse, *Bertha*—but out stepped a teenage girl.

Her dark hair was tied back, her pale skin nearly glowed in the sunlight, and the hem of her brown dress was just a little too long. It dragged across the branch as she walked, barefoot, with a wooden pail pressed against her hip.

Mihi stepped away, trying to hide behind the trunk—but she wasn't quick enough. The girl spotted her.

As soon as she saw Mihi, her mouth fell open. She dropped the pail, and water spilled down the tree trunk. Mihi could practically *see* the scream frozen in the girl's throat.

Mihi didn't know who—or what—else lived in the village, but she couldn't ignore that squirming fear in her gut. There was something dangerous here. And if this girl called out, she might summon it.

"Wait." Mihi held up her hands. "I'm sorry. I was just leaving. Please don't call anyone."

The girl blinked quickly. Then she started climbing down, swinging and hopping between branches so effortlessly that it made Mihi dizzy.

The girl jumped from the final branch and landed barefoot on the grass, just a few feet from Mihi.

"*Wow*," the girl said, staring at Mihi as if she were a science experiment.

Suddenly Mihi felt very, very uncomfortable. "Sorry," she repeated. "I just . . ."

The girl took a step forward—now inches from Mihi's face. This close, Mihi could see the emotions flitting through the girl's eyes: caution, confusion, surprise, and then, slowly . . . delight. A closed-lip smile

bloomed across the girl's face, and she raised a single brow before declaring: "You're a Grey."

Mihi stepped back. Nobody in the castle had been able to tell she was a Grey just by looking. "How did you . . . ?"

The girl flashed a grin. "I'm a witch."

When Mihi took another step back, the girl laughed. "Just kidding," she said.

But Mihi wasn't quite convinced.

"My name's Maven. I have a mirror that gives me hints about stuff that will happen," the girl went on. "Like a fortune-teller, but with riddles."

There were plenty of magic mirrors in fairy tales, but one stood out. Mihi swallowed. Her initial fear sharpened. Though she wasn't certain, though she could have been totally and completely wrong, she was starting to suspect that she was standing right in front of Snow White's evil queen.

Chapter 19

"My magic mirror told me I should help you," Maven said. "So how can I help?"

"Uh," Mihi hesitated. Her stomach flipped. *Could this be Snow White's evil queen?* But that made no sense. This girl seemed so *nice*, and she was too young.

Wiping her sweating palms on her dress, Mihi said, "You don't need to help me. I've finally figured out where I'm going. Thanks, though."

Mihi gave a half wave as she backed up, the universal sign for *please leave me alone now*. But when she turned to walk away, Maven followed.

"Where are you going?" she asked, grinning. She either didn't notice that Mihi was trying to ditch her, or she didn't care.

"The Healing Orchard," Mihi told her. What else

could she do? This girl was going to follow her whether she liked it or not.

Maven's voice bubbled with giddiness. "I grew up hearing stories about that orchard. But nobody's used it for ages."

"Why not?"

"We're not allowed. And the rules in the Rainbow Realm are strictly enforced—even though an orchard would help my village a lot. It's not easy living in the forest."

Mihi frowned. "It isn't?"

Maven shrugged. "Nope. We're not important enough, so nobody cares about helping us. We have to fend for ourselves, which is fine in the summer. But in the winter, food can be scarce. Even though the castles have a ton."

"Oh," Mihi murmured. She thought of Sleeping Beauty's feasts. So much food, more than one person could ever eat. Did the princess know about any of this?

Maven tilted her head. "So, what brings you to the orchard?"

"I—" In many ways, Mihi understood this girl

better than she'd understood the princess. *We're not important enough.* But still, something stopped Mihi from trusting her. She couldn't tell a possible evil witch about Reese and Savannah. "I have a hunch it might help, and I hope I'm right."

"I have a hunch too." Maven's eyes narrowed, and Mihi shivered under her gaze. "My mirror said I'd find someone like me one day, and I think you're that person."

Mihi blinked. "What makes you think that?"

"I can always sense the desperate types. Some people have to work harder than everyone else, because the game is rigged against us. We can't just *get* what we want." She lifted a brow. "And if you can't get what you want, are you willing to take it?"

Mihi took a step backward. "I . . . I don't know."

"Then let's find out." She reached into her pocket, pulled out a key, and dangled it in front of Mihi. "The door to the orchard is locked. For *most* people. But a magic mirror can be helpful in lots of ways. You end up with a lot of things nobody intended for you to have."

Alarm bells went off in Mihi's head. Breaking into

the orchard seemed like a bad idea, as did trusting this girl. But this time, when Maven started walking, Mihi followed. What choice did she have? She needed to find a way in.

They walked the dirt path out of the forest and toward the orchard, and when they arrived, the girl unlocked the iron gate and pushed it open, revealing a grove rich with color.

"Wow," Mihi murmured.

On each fruit tree hung a sign describing its special healing ability. Peaches for heartbreak. Sour cherries for jealousy. Hot chocolate for brain freeze.

"Hot chocolate?" Mihi squinted at the tree, trying to make sense of it. Steaming mugs seemed to grow right out of the leaves.

Maven laughed. "You coming?"

Mihi followed her inside, past trees full of lemons and oranges and sugarplums. Past fruits that claimed to heal nightmares and headaches and temper tantrums. Along the way, she found a pear tree that appeared to bear normal, unenchanted fruit, so she slipped some into her pockets for her friends to eat.

Then she saw it—right there, right in the corner, a tree that looked almost identical to the one at Mihi's school. On a branch hung the sign: *Apples, for broken bones and broken hearts.*

"That's exactly what I need," Mihi whispered as she ran toward it and began to climb.

Mihi climbed higher and higher, hair blowing in the wind. If this had happened a day ago, Mihi might have recalled her climb at school. She might have remembered how she'd reached the highest branches. She might have heard the echo of Genevieve's words.

But now, Mihi wasn't thinking about any of that. As she climbed, branch by branch, as she plucked the apple, fresh and red and perfect, the only thing she thought about was Savannah. Her friend needed her.

After she'd climbed back down, apple safely in hand, Mihi said, "I have to go."

"That's too bad. I hope to see you again," Maven said, eyes sparkling as she looked at Mihi's apple. She wore an expression that unsettled Mihi, but Mihi didn't have time to focus on that. Every moment she was gone, Savannah was in pain. Every moment she was gone, Bertha got closer.

She had to get back.

But as she was leaving, Maven called out, "Are you headed to the Just Right Home Cottage?"

Mihi turned. In truth, she didn't know where they were going after this. She'd been hoping that Reese had formed a plan. But maybe this girl could help. "Where's that?"

"It's a few miles from here. You just have to go through the Wood of Nightmares," she said, as casually as one might say, *you just have to pop down to Costco*.

"Oh, don't be such a worrywart," she added, seeing Mihi's expression. "You can skirt the very edge of it, without traveling into the heart of the Wood. As long as you find the river, you'll be fine. Follow it until you see a little brick cottage covered in ivy."

Mihi hesitated. She needed to go. And anything that led them through the Wood of Nightmares clearly wasn't a good idea. "Why should I go to the Just Right Home Cottage?"

A sly grin stretched across Maven's lips. "Because it's the place to go if you want answers. There was a Grey there, once. And she managed to do something impossible."

Impossible. The word lifted the hair on Mihi's neck, like it always did. "What did she do?"

"Well, the thing every Grey wants. She made her own fairy tale. And if that's what you want, are you willing to take it?"

Chapter 20

Mihi almost walked right by Reese and Savannah. It wasn't until Reese called Mihi's name that Mihi noticed them. Reese had done an incredible job camouflaging the little cave. She'd gathered leaves and branches to cover it, and had even dragged a big rock to block most of the cave's entrance.

Mihi ran to her friends, dropping to her knees beside Savannah as she pulled the apple from her pocket. "It's for broken bones," she explained.

Savannah took the apple, turning it over in her palms.

"Do you think it's safe?" Reese asked. "It could have an entirely different chemical makeup than apples in our world."

Mihi hesitated. "Reese has a point. Apples in

fairy tales don't always have the best results. It could be dangerous."

Savannah swallowed. "If it means I'll be able to walk, then it's worth the risk. I don't want to hold you two back."

"You aren't holding us back," Mihi said firmly.

Reese nodded. "We're in this together."

They squeezed Savannah's hands, and Savannah took a bite. Mihi held her breath, willing this to work, hoping beyond hope that she hadn't delivered poison right to her friend's lips.

And then Savannah screamed. The apple fell to the ground with a thud.

"Savannah!" Mihi shouted.

Savannah grabbed her ankle, which had begun to glow. Reese rushed to inspect it, and Savannah squeezed Mihi's wrist, cutting off all circulation.

"Oh no," Reese breathed.

Then the glow began to subside. Savannah gulped air. Her grip on Mihi loosened.

"Are you okay?" Mihi whispered.

Reese held Savannah's ankle, gently examining it.

"It looks . . . better," she said, stunned and cautious. "It looks good, actually."

And it did. It looked like it had never been broken in the first place.

Marveling, Savannah rolled out her ankle. And then, very slowly, she stood, testing her weight.

She took one step. Then another.

Mihi let out her breath.

"This is perfect," Reese said. "Now we can get going."

"I actually met someone when I was getting that apple," Mihi said. "And she suggested that we go to a place called the Just Right Home Cottage."

Mihi pointed as Reese unfurled the map, but before she could explain that this was where Greys went to create their own fairy tales, Reese looked up and grinned.

"Of course!" she exclaimed. "The *Just Right Home Cottage*. It'll take us right home. Mihi, that's genius."

"I'm not sure—" Mihi began.

But Reese turned to Savannah. "Do you feel better enough to walk?"

Savannah threw her arms wide and belted into a loud, off-pitch song. *"I do feel better, I do! Reese, Mihi, how can I ever thank you?"*

Instantly, Savannah's eyes went wide, and she clapped her hands over her mouth. Reese and Mihi simply stared.

"Savannah," Mihi said carefully. "You know I love a good song. Really, I think it's great. But, uh . . ."

"I thought you hated singing," Reese finished.

"I really, truly hate my voice, but I don't think I have a choice." Savannah *was* rather off-key, but the worst part was that she looked physically pained when she sang.

Reese and Mihi exchanged a glance.

"The sign," Mihi said, attempting to make sense of this, "it said 'for broken bones and broken hearts.'"

"But why would that make her sing?" Reese asked.

Mihi shook her head, lost.

"Oh," Savannah murmured, a single, sorrowful note. *"Broken hearts. Where do I even start?"*

Reese and Mihi waited, and Savannah took a deep breath, gathering the courage to sing again.

"When I was small, I loved to sing.
I even adored practicing.
So I tried out for the play last year.
I'd get a role—I had no fear!
But, woe! I did not get the part.
The other kids, they broke my heart.
They said I couldn't be the star,
I locked my dreams into a jar.
I vowed to never sing again,
and that is how this sad song ends."

"Savannah," Mihi whispered. "That's heartbreaking. If you love to sing, you should sing! You shouldn't care what anyone else thinks."

Savannah bit her lip, afraid to sing again.

Reese spoke up. "Of course she cares. We *all* care. That's why we're here, isn't it?"

Mihi stared at Reese. "What do you mean?"

"That's the whole point of being a princess. So other people like us more. But I'm tired of trying to fit in. I just want to go home."

"So even if there was still a chance to have our own

fairy tale, without a horrible competition, or annoying training, or evil death weeds," Mihi asked, "you wouldn't want it?"

Reese shook her head. So did Savannah.

Mihi took a step back. It was like they'd shot a blob of grey icing right at Mihi's sparkling fantasy. Being a princess wasn't *just* about making people like her. At least, Mihi didn't think it was. It was so much more than that. Being a princess was about the *perfect life*. It was . . . well, it was what Mihi always wanted. It was Mihi's dream! And though she couldn't quite explain *why* anymore, a dream should be reason enough!

She'd thought she found people who understood her, but Reese and Savannah . . . didn't.

Savannah's eyes filled with sympathy. *"I know how much this means to you, but we must bid this world adieu."*

Reese nodded. "Savannah's right. I'm sure going home will fix this singing spell too. We have to get to the Just Right Home Cottage."

Mihi hesitated. She knew she should tell them what the girl had said. She knew this cottage might not be what they thought it was. They deserved to know.

But . . . this had been Mihi's dream for so long.

She'd thought she had to give it up. She'd thought she was silly to want it. But what if that wasn't true? Maybe the mice or Bertha weren't going to hand her dream to her, but maybe, at this cottage, she could take it. Maybe this was just another challenge, and a true princess would rise to the occasion.

Her conscience whispered, warning her not to lie, but she *wasn't* lying. She just wasn't saying everything. And anyway, Maven told her this was a place to go for *answers*. Maybe, if they went there, they'd also find out how to cure Savannah of song and how to get her friends home.

This could work out for everyone. This could be easy.

Mihi forced a smile. "Exactly."

Chapter 21

They were lost.

They were lost in the Wood of Nightmares.

As soon as they'd entered, Mihi realized that the name was no joke. Unlike the bright colors and warm moss of the forest, the trees in the wood looked dead. No color, no leaves, just dark black branches reaching into the sky, tangling together, blocking out the sun.

Worse, were the eyes.

Mihi could *feel* them. Eyes everywhere, all around her, all *on* her—invisible aside from the skin-slither of being *watched*.

If these were the outskirts of the Wood, she didn't even want to think about the heart of it.

"An awful space, I hate this place," Savannah

whisper-sang, after they'd been walking for what felt like hours.

"Me too," Mihi whispered back. Something scuttled along the branches overhead and Mihi shivered. But she told herself that this was just the *adventure* part of becoming a princess. Lots of princesses had to struggle before finding their happily ever after. *Just keep moving*, she told herself. *Don't question it.*

Reese consulted the map and let out a long hiss of defeat. "I'm pretty sure we just walked in a circle. Twice."

Savannah looked close to tears, but she clamped her hand over her mouth, determined not to sing.

Reese frowned. "According to wilderness safety, you're supposed to stay in one place so people can find you. But nobody's looking for us."

"Some people are!" Mihi said.

"Okay, fine," Reese corrected. "Some people are looking for us. So they can kill us."

"We'll be okay," Mihi insisted. "We just have to keep walking."

"In what direction?" Reese asked.

Mihi pulled the compass out of her pocket. It wasn't the first time she'd tried it, but that needle kept spinning and spinning. The compass seemed as lost as they were. "I don't know where Stonington is, but apparently they make awful compasses," she said.

"We thought this would be safe, but we see that was a lie. We must escape this place, or else . . ." Savannah's voice grew louder as her panic rose, and she struggled to keep her lips clamped, but the words burst through anyway. *"Or else . . . we'll surely . . . DIE!"*

Savannah clapped her hand over her mouth, but it was too late. All around them, yellow eyes blinked awake.

In the distance they heard the howl of a wolf, and Mihi went cold. Wolves in real life were scary—but wolves in fairy tales were terrifying.

The bushes in front of them rustled and shook. Mihi's heart roared in her ears. She grasped for her friends' hands.

Then something flew out of the leaves.

Reese screamed.

Mihi squeezed her eyes shut.

Seconds ticked by . . . and she hadn't been swallowed whole. Cracking her eyes back open, Mihi saw a small brown toad squatting in front of them.

She could have fainted with relief. Reese let out a long, shaky breath.

And Savannah leaned toward it. *"Oh, hello,"* she sang, her voice going high and sweet, as if she were talking to a puppy.

"Savannah," Reese whispered. "Don't scare it off. We might be able to eat it."

Mihi squished her nose. "I'm not *that* hungry," she said, though her stomach growled in protest. They'd eaten the pears from the orchard, which thankfully hadn't had any musical side effects, but the fruit wasn't nearly enough.

"Don't *eat* me," the toad ribbited.

All three girls scrambled back, and Reese cried, *"This* animal talks too?"

"Don't sound so surprised," the toad scolded, and Mihi had to admit he had a point. "And if you must know, Stonington is in a world called Mane."

Mihi frowned. "Mane? Like a horse? Is that near here?"

"Not sure," the toad replied. "I heard about it from a girl, a long time ago. Toads live many years. Much longer than *frogs*."

"It's true, my dears," Savannah whisper-sang. *"They can live for, like, forty years."*

"Longer," the toad croaked.

"Mane . . ." Reese murmured. "Do you think he could possibly mean Maine? Like the state?"

Mihi frowned. "But that's in *our* world. How would a compass from *Maine* have gotten here—and into my pocket?"

Reese shook her head. "I don't know."

"Now, move," the toad said, irritable and impatient. "You're in my way."

Mihi stepped aside, but Savannah rushed in

to fill her spot, blocking his path. *"I don't mean to be a bother, but toads live close to water!"*

"That means the river!" Mihi exclaimed. "It must be close."

"Can you show us the way?" Reese asked.

The toad narrowed his eyes. "I don't have time for humans. You ask so much from animals, but care so little. None of you pay attention to the ways of toads."

Savannah's eyes lit up.

"I know more than we were taught!
A group of toads is called a knot.
You're called a tadpole when you're young
and as you age you grow a tongue.
You have no teeth, that takes a toll,
so what you eat you swallow whole.
And sometimes, when you feel boxed in,
your glands release bufotoxin!"

The toad stared at her. As did Reese. As did Mihi. For the first time, Savannah didn't look pained as she sang. She looked . . . happy. She glowed.

"Wow," said Reese, finally.

"This human is strange," the toad responded. "But admirable. Follow me."

He hopped through the woods, and the girls ran to keep up.

"Why do you know so many toad facts?" Reese panted, as they chased him.

"My grandpa loved amphibians. I spent a lot of time with him," Savannah said, seeming, now, quite happy to sing. *"He lived with us for many years, and always helped me soothe my fears."*

Mihi didn't know any other kids whose grandparents lived with them, and knowing this made her feel just a little closer to Savannah.

Before long they reached the river, a sparkling rush of water that sounded almost musical. And as they stepped closer, Mihi realized it *was* music. It was a melody she almost recognized—something that felt familiar, like the warmth of her flannel bedsheets, or the scent of kimchi jjigae on a winter day, or the barking of new puppies at the shelter. Like *home.*

"Don't step any closer," the toad advised.

Mihi blinked, surprised to find that she had edged her way to the bank of the river—so close that the water ran over the toes of her shoes. "Thanks," she murmured.

"And don't drink the water, or you'll be sorry. I hope you can swim," he said, before hopping away.

"Why do we need to swim?" Mihi called after him.

But they found out soon enough, because the mud shifted beneath their feet—and then it gave way, sweeping them into the water.

As a little kid, Mihi had hated swimming lessons. She disliked putting her head underwater, and she was always, always, the slowest swimmer in class. She'd begged her mom to let her quit. They were miles from the ocean, after all.

But her mother had insisted. *One day*, she'd told Mihi, *you'll thank me.*

And as it turned out, that day was today.

The current moved quickly—so different than Mihi's safe community swimming pool—and Mihi tumbled beneath the waves. River water shot up her nose, plugged her ears, and burned her eyes, but she kept her lips pressed tightly together, and she kicked.

Mihi kicked like her life depended on it because, well, *it did.* And finally, as her lungs exploded against her chest, her head burst through the surface.

She gulped air, sucking oxygen into her burning lungs.

Bursting up beside her, Savannah gasped before the river dragged her back under.

"Savannah!" Mihi called out. She fought against the current, fought to stay above water, but Savannah didn't reemerge.

There was no time to think. Mihi dove back in, eyes burning and blurry as she opened them underwater. The waves tumbled and tossed her, so she no longer knew which way was up—and then she saw Savannah. Her dress was caught on a rock, and she was struggling to free herself.

Mihi kicked as hard as she could, reaching for her friend. The waves were strong. But Mihi found that she was strong too.

Her lungs threatened to rebel, but she wrapped her arms around Savannah's waist and tugged. The skirt of Savannah's dress ripped, revealing pants underneath, and the two girls swam desperately toward the sky.

When they broke the surface, Mihi breathed

deeply, adrenaline and oxygen surging through her veins. "Where's Reese?"

Savannah's eyes grew wide, and they called out, searching for their friend, but the roaring river drowned their cries.

No, no, no.

Mihi prepared to dive again, but then she heard Reese scream, "Look out!"

Mihi found Reese clinging to a tree root on the riverbank and pointing downstream—at rocks. Sharp, jagged, piercing rocks. Just a few yards ahead, water smashed against stone, slamming with bone-rattling force.

"Oh dear," Savannah gasped as she fought against the current. *"There's so much to fear."*

"Grab my hand!" Reese cried.

Swallowing some water seemed like the least of their worries, but Mihi kept her mouth clamped shut anyway. Frantically, desperately, Mihi and Savannah swam.

If Mihi survived this, she would thank her mother a hundred times. A million times. She would *never stop thanking her mother.* She missed her mother. She missed home. She missed it so much it hurt.

With one final push, Mihi's fingers brushed against Reese's, and they clasped hands.

"Keep kicking," Reese grunted, as she pulled Mihi toward her.

Mihi reached back and grabbed Savannah's hand. Her arms stretched wide between Reese and Savannah, like the river was playing tug-of-war.

"I'm trying." Mihi's muscles burned, but she didn't let up.

Reese managed to pull herself onto the riverbank, and she tugged Mihi up after her. Together, they pulled Savannah out of the water.

On the safety of land, all three of them collapsed, muscles aching, hearts thumping.

"We're alive," Mihi marveled.

"Seems that way," Reese breathed. Her tight bun had mostly come undone, and loose curls dripped over her shoulders. A few remaining bobby pins stuck out from her hair. "Let's never do that again," she said, as she wrung out her skirt.

"I'd be okay with that," Mihi agreed.

Savannah stood, pushing a curtain of wet hair from her face, and squinted at something in the distance.

Mihi peered through the trees. Sure enough, she saw a little brick cottage with ivy creeping up the walls.

"Is that it?" Reese asked. "Our way home?"

Mihi frowned. Seeing her friends in so much danger had changed things. She couldn't put them at risk. Not anymore.

"I'm not sure . . ." Mihi began.

"It has to be," Savannah said, teeth chattering. Her pants dripped, turning the dirt beneath her into mud. *"It said 'home,' you see."*

"That's true, but . . ." Mihi tried.

"We came all this way," Reese said. "We almost *drowned* trying to find this place."

Mihi hesitated. She had to tell them. "The girl at the orchard told me to come here," she made herself say. "But . . ."

Reese froze, hearing the sorrow in Mihi's tone. Savannah chewed her lip.

"But when I asked her if this was our way home . . . it didn't sound like it."

Reese blinked. "What did it sound like?"

Mihi's voice cracked, barely audible. "She said it was a place where Greys could make our own fairy tales."

Reese's eyes burned. "But we don't *want* to make our own fairy tales. We *want* to go home."

"*Mihi,*" Savannah sang softly. "*This was our only hope. If we can't go home, I don't know how I'll cope.*"

"We're stuck here, Sav." Reese refused to meet Mihi's eyes. "Because Mihi lied."

The looks on her friends' faces were impossible to bear. Mihi had messed up. She'd put all of them in danger. And for what?

She'd been running so fast, chasing this dream. She'd been so focused on the person she *wanted* to be that she hadn't even considered the person she was *actually* being. And she was being selfish.

"I'm so, so sorry," Mihi whispered. "But . . . I don't know for sure. Maybe this really *is* a way home. The orchard girl said something about answers, I think. So maybe this is a portal. If a refrigerator could be a portal, then this cottage could too. Right?"

Reese's face hardened. For a long time, her friends

did not respond. Mihi bit her cheek so she wouldn't cry.

Helplessly, Savannah looked between the two of them. *"We're stuck. Without bufotoxin, we're out of luck."*

Reese met Mihi's eyes, and Mihi could tell—Reese didn't trust her. But Savannah was right. They were out of options.

Reese said, "Fine. Let's check it out. Mihi, you first."

Mihi inhaled, deeply, before walking through the trees and up to the cottage door.

When she knocked, the door creaked open, like it was inviting them in. And Mihi stepped forward, crossing the threshold.

Chapter 23

The cottage was not too small, not too big—just enough space for a kitchen and three beds. It definitely didn't seem like a portal back to their world.

"Where are we?" Reese murmured.

Around them, the room was lit with candles that cast shadows into corners and filled the air with the scent of cinnamon.

"Come. Make yourself at home." A rasping voice echoed around them, and Mihi felt the words rattling inside her, like claws scratching against bone.

From the shadows, a hulking figure emerged—and as it stepped into the light, Mihi saw: a bear. A giant brown bear, with matted fur and sharp claws.

Mihi stumbled backward and Reese darted for the door, but it slammed shut behind them.

"You wouldn't want to offend your hosts." The bear's voice sounded like the scrape kitchen knives made when Mihi's mom sharpened them.

"Um," Mihi stammered, her own voice cracking with fear. "No, no, of course not. Which is why we don't want to—to intrude."

A slightly smaller black bear stepped out from behind him, followed by an even smaller black bear— this one still a cub. Mihi had a pretty good guess which fairy tale they belonged to, and it didn't make her feel much better.

"What are you doing in our cottage?" the medium bear asked.

Mihi cleared her throat. "We're just lost." Days ago, she'd said the same thing to the mice at the Information Booth. The words seemed even truer now.

"Nobody is ever just lost," the brown bear said, teeth glinting. "There is always more to the story."

Mihi glanced at the smallest bear, the little cub, but he slunk back into the shadows. There was more to his story—Mihi felt certain about that.

"Please, have a seat," the medium bear said, her eyes unreadable. "You look tired."

The baby bear stepped forward and gestured to the three beds in front of them. The girls didn't appear to have a choice, so they sat, one on each bed.

Mihi's heart began to tumble, torn between two pressing concerns. On the one hand, they had to get out of there. Fast.

On the other, Mihi couldn't stop thinking about what the girl had said. If this was a place for answers, would they know how to cure Savannah? Would they know how to get home?

And of course, there was that nagging question Mihi still couldn't quite let go of. Because if the orchard girl was telling the truth, this was where a Grey created her own story. Could Mihi ask the bears about that? Would her friends ever forgive her if she did?

"You look hungry too," the medium bear added, as she lumbered over to the kitchen and stirred a boiling pot with a wooden spoon.

"Oh, that's okay. We're not—" Mihi began.

But the big brown bear interrupted. "My wife is kind. You will eat what she gives you."

That didn't sound like a choice either.

The medium bear spooned a lump of grey sludge

into three bowls and carried them over on a metal tray. As Mihi took her bowl, it seemed to radiate warmth— spreading into her hands and through her body— and when she looked inside, she realized what it was. Porridge.

"*Goldilocks's bears!*" Mihi confirmed her hunch. Even now, when she was 60 percent sure they were about to devour her, this was amazing: she was meeting *the three bears.*

"We do not belong to *Goldilocks,*" the black bear snarled.

"*Eat!*" the brown bear demanded.

So Mihi and her friends spooned the porridge into their mouths. It was too hot, but Mihi ate anyway. She hadn't realized how hungry she was. Fleeing from death took a lot of energy.

And it was delicious, so much better than it looked, perfectly soothing and honey-sweet. By the time she finished, she already wanted more.

Reese and Savannah ate their bowls quickly too.

It tasted almost like red bean rice cakes, but when Mihi turned to tell her friends, Savannah's brows pinched and she whispered, "Does it taste like beef jerky to you?"

Then she blinked. "I didn't sing!"

The medium bear leaned forward, looming. "Feel better?"

Savannah nodded, eyes wide, and Mihi had to agree.

She felt rested and energized and safe—but there was another feeling too, swirling beneath the surface. An unsettling, buzzing sensation that she couldn't name.

The black bear's lips lifted into something close to a smile. Mihi had never seen a bear smile before, and she wasn't sure if it was comforting or scary. "My porridge is famous throughout the land. It'll warm you and comfort you and cure most magical ailments. It's the dash of homesickness that does it. Powerful magic, in small doses."

Reese frowned. "Homesickness?"

"I only add a few drops from the Homesick River. Just a touch, not too much."

Mihi looked at her friends. The river. The toad told them not to drink from it—or they'd be sorry.

"Homesickness isn't a fun emotion to feel, of course," the bear continued, "but people are always drawn to it. For many, remembering the past is easier than facing the future."

Savannah tucked a strand of hair behind her ear. "Even if they have a happily ever after?"

The baby bear spoke softly. "Not everyone in this land gets a happily ever after. And not everybody wants their story to end."

Mihi lowered her bowl. She thought of Maven, who lived a life of hunger while food went to waste in the castle. And she thought, too, of Sleeping Beauty, trapped and lonely, destined to marry a prince she didn't like and live a life she never wanted. Neither seemed so happily ever after.

The big brown bear spoke again, shaking Mihi from her thoughts. "The homesickness can be useful to us too. It taps into people's emotions. And when people are emotional, they are honest. So, tell us: Why would three little girls end up at our cottage when everybody in this land knows to avoid it?"

Reese turned to glare at Mihi, and Mihi winced,

but none of them spoke. They knew not to trust these bears.

And yet, Mihi . . . missed home. She missed it so badly that suddenly, she couldn't think of anything else. Home was so much more important than any fantasy. Home was real.

Tears spilled from her eyes and, to her horror, words poured from her lips.

"We came here by accident and we stayed because we wanted to be special—*I* wanted to be special—but I put my friends in danger and ruined everything." Mihi clamped her lips together and turned to her friends in apology, but they seemed to be having the same oversharing problem.

"You call our world the Grey World," Reese blurted, voice choked with feeling. "But it's not grey at all. We have laws of physics and rules of the universe—unlike here. And I wanted to stay in your world for a while, to learn about it, but now I just want to leave. And I'm really, really mad at Mihi, even though I don't want to be."

Mihi looked at Reese, surprised by this, but all she

saw in Reese's eyes was panic. Neither of them could make sense of why they were confessing. All Mihi knew was that she felt helpless, drowning in home-sickness. She wanted her mom. She wanted those red bean rice cakes and her bed and the soft warmth of home.

A sob burst from Savannah's lips. "We're trying to get back home. We need to get back home. Can you help us?"

The black bear sighed. "Unfortunately, there's no way back."

Mihi felt like she couldn't breathe.

Reese wiped at the flood of tears and tried to steady her voice. "But there has to be. If there's a way in, there's a way out."

Mihi nodded. "And the mice told us there was a way."

The brown bear's lip curled in disgust. "Those awful mice love chaos and resent Greys. Maybe they were looking for a bit of fun, served with a side of revenge."

Savannah's voice shook. "So, we can never go back home?"

"That can't be *it*," Mihi said. Her brain felt staticky. Her mouth got fuzzy and her fingers went tingly. Maybe it was the fear getting to her. "You're supposed to have answers."

The brown bear smiled, and Mihi decided that yes, bears smiling was terrifying. "Sorry, Greys. We can't help you."

For some reason, Mihi couldn't form words. Her brain wasn't working right. And she was getting so sleepy . . .

"What did you do to us?" Reese's voice sounded fuzzy too.

"We added a little nightleaf in addition to the homesickness." The brown bear's voice drifted around them. "We don't *want* to hurt you. If there was a way back, we'd tell you. But since there isn't, we can't risk having Greys in our world. We don't exactly trust your kind."

"We're really very sorry," his wife added.

And the world went black.

Chapter 24

Mihi woke to cold and darkness. Her body ached and a groan escaped her lips, echoing in the dark. She blinked, waiting for her eyes to adjust, but the world stayed black.

Beneath her, the floor was cold and hard—and her hands were tied behind her back. When she tried to pull free, cool metal bit into her wrists. She was chained to the wall.

"Reese? Savannah?" she whispered.

Reese groaned. "We just got poisoned by talking bears."

Savannah moaned. "I'm never eating anything in this world ever again."

Relief swept over Mihi. They were still together. They were still alive.

"Can you slip out of the chains?" Mihi asked.

The sound of clanging metal echoed, followed by Savannah's voice: "No."

Mihi tugged harder against the chains, but they wouldn't budge.

"What do we do?" Mihi asked, her voice verging on total panic.

She heard Reese gulp. "Wait to be disposed of?"

Mihi had never heard Reese sound so defeated, and when she *clang-clang-clang*ed again without any luck, Mihi's heart swelled with dread.

They would never escape this place.

"I made a terrible mistake," Mihi told her friends. "I knew you wouldn't want to come here if I told you it was where Greys came to make their own fairy tales, so I lied. But if lying and hurting my friends was the cost of getting that dream, then I don't think the dream was worth it. I'm so sorry. I should have told you the truth."

Reese and Savannah whispered to each other, and finally Reese said, "Yes, you should have."

"But you wanted so badly to believe," Savannah said softly.

Mihi's heart crunched. Of course she had. How

was it that even in this magical fairy-tale realm, where anything and everything seemed possible, Mihi *still* couldn't be the princess type?

Reese sighed. "I'm mad, but . . . I know what it's like to want to believe."

"Just don't lie to us again," Savannah added.

Mihi hesitated, almost too afraid to ask. "Can you ever forgive me?"

"Maybe," Reese said.

"If we get out of here, I'll always be honest with you," Mihi said. "I promise."

But one crucial word seemed to echo around them. *If.* If they got out.

And the truth was . . . Reese and Savannah would never get the chance to forgive her, because they'd never escape.

Just as despair threatened to swallow Mihi whole, a door creaked open. A crack of light split the room, and Mihi saw that they were trapped in a dungeon.

An actual *dungeon.*

Which, honestly, would have been kind of cool—if they weren't facing certain death.

"*Quiet*," a voice hissed.

It took a second for Mihi to realize it was the little bear cub.

"My parents are going to hear you," he said.

Mihi heard the *flick-hiss* of a match being lit, and then a small candle filled the dungeon with sneering shadows. The cub stepped inside.

"Let us out of here!" Mihi cried.

"Hush, please. I'm trying to help. My name is Blackberry." He slipped a weathered leather backpack off his shoulders. "I brought you some porridge," he said, pulling a thermos out of the bag. "And some water and fruit, in case you're hungry."

"Uh, we definitely don't want more porridge," Reese said.

"I made a batch without the nightleaf, so it won't knock you out," he said. "I'm trying to help."

Fear and frustration rose in Mihi's throat and came out tasting bitter. "Last time your family 'helped,' we ended up in a *dungeon*."

Savannah cleared her throat. "What Mihi's trying to say is, will you please set us free?"

"And stop your parents from eating us?" Reese added.

Blackberry frowned. "You have to understand, my parents aren't bad people. They mean well, but they're stuck in their old ways."

Reese shook her head. "Lots of people mean well, but they don't *do* well."

"Especially when their old ways mean locking children in a dungeon and eating them," Mihi added.

Blackberry winced. "They don't *necessarily* want to eat you. They'll decide in the morning if they should let the mice deal with you, or if they should . . ."

"Eat us," Savannah finished.

Blackberry sighed. "They don't realize they have other options."

The girls exchanged a glance, and Reese asked, carefully, "*Are* there other options?"

The baby bear swallowed. "I've heard rumors. They're only rumors, so I'm not sure. But there might be a way for you to get home."

The metal cuffs dug into Mihi's wrists as she leaned forward. "How?"

When he paused, Mihi begged, "Please, Blackberry. If there's another way, please help us. I know you might have grown up thinking there was one way you were supposed to be, that there were rules you had to follow to fit in. But . . . you can make your own path."

He swallowed.

"You don't have to be like your parents," Savannah added.

In the candlelight, Mihi could see the fear flickering in Blackberry's eyes. But she saw the determination too. He nodded. "Legend has it that when the Greys built walls between our worlds, everything changed. They were trapped there. We were trapped here. No way in. No way out."

"But . . ." Reese said. "*We* got in."

"Exactly. That's the official story, but there are . . . gaps in that story. A few people, like you, have gone between worlds. So some of us believe that as the walls were being built, a group of Greys and 'Bows worked together to hide a few doors, scattered throughout the land. If you found one of them, maybe you could go back."

"So we just have to find a hidden door," Mihi said, "like we found the refrigerator."

It sounded simple. All they had to do was find a door. This was perfect—or at least, it was as perfect as they could hope for, considering they were trapped in a dungeon with a growing list of people who wanted to kill them.

"How do you know all this?" Savannah asked.

Blackberry hesitated. "I overheard my parents talking once, when I was just a tiny cub. They said Goldilocks was a Grey."

Mihi's ears rang with the revelation. Goldilocks was a Grey. *Goldilocks was a Grey.* But that was impossible . . . unless the orchard girl had been right. Unless a Grey really had managed to create her own story—and one of the biggest stories, at that.

This changed everything. Mihi turned to her friends, eager to see their reactions, but they were both fixated on Blackberry.

"Do you know where those hidden doors are?" Reese asked.

And with that, Mihi realized this *didn't* change

anything. At least, it didn't change anything for her friends. And that meant it couldn't change anything for her either. She owed it to them to prioritize getting home—no matter how much she wanted to know about Goldilocks.

The bear sighed. "I've heard some speculation about where the doors are, but it's not so simple. Even if you *did* find one, you'd still have to activate it. And nobody knows how."

"But it's possible?" Mihi asked. "We have a chance?"

"I think so. I've heard of four doors, and one of them may be hidden in Sleeping Beauty's castle, which is near here."

Mihi's stomach flipped. The good news: They knew the castle well, so they'd have an advantage when searching for the door.

The bad news: They'd be walking right back to another place where people wanted them dead.

Lovely.

Mihi turned to her friends. "We can do this," she said. They nodded.

To Blackberry, Savannah said, "Thank you. From the bottom of our hearts. Now, if you unlock us, we'll be on our way and forever grateful."

Blackberry winced. "Oh," he said. "I forgot. I don't have the key. My parents keep it hidden."

All the excitement rushed out of Mihi. They were trapped here after all. The bears would eat them and—

Reese cleared her throat, eyes narrowed with focus. "I have an idea."

Chapter 25

"Blackberry," Reese said, "I'm gonna need you to pull a few of these bobby pins from my hair. Careful, please."

Slowly, Blackberry pulled three pins from Reese's curls. The girls watched as he struggled to hold them between his claws.

"This might be harder than I thought," Reese said. But she took a deep breath. "First, slide one of the pins into the keyhole of these handcuffs."

Reese adjusted herself as much as she could so Blackberry could reach her wrists.

Again, the bear did as he was told. Again, his claws made this challenging.

"All right, I got the first pin," he finally told her.

Reese nodded once, all business. Her glasses slid down her nose as sweat trickled down her face, and

Mihi watched with awe. Reese, the smartest person Mihi knew. Reese, who could fix—and take apart—anything. Reese, who might just save them from this mess.

"Okay, now for the second pin. There should be a much smaller hole on the other side of the lock—stick the pin in there."

Blackberry nodded. "Got it."

"And now the third pin," Reese continued. "That's the trickiest of all. You'll have to stick it into the lock, right above the first pin, and just kind of . . . wiggle it. You'll start to feel some clicking. That's a good thing. Keep going. Keep tilting the pin up."

Mihi and Savannah watched, holding their breaths as Blackberry worked. Hoping, hoping, hoping—until they heard a soft *click*, followed by a clatter as Reese's handcuffs fell to the floor.

Blackberry blinked, like he could hardly believe it. "You did it," he whispered.

"*We* did it." Reese blew out hot relief. "I've done that once before when I accidentally locked myself out of my room. But this was a totally different level."

She grabbed the pins and got to work on her

friends. She moved much faster than the bear, first freeing Savannah's chains, then Mihi's.

Mihi rubbed her bare wrists. Giddiness pumped in her chest. "You're amazing." She grinned, throwing her arms around Reese.

Savannah tossed herself into the hug. "You saved us."

"Don't get too excited. We still have a murderous lady-in-waiting to face and a hidden door to find," Reese responded. But she was grinning as she pulled the last few pins from her hair and shook out her curls.

Blackberry knelt and lifted a piece of the floor, revealing a trapdoor. "This way," he said, handing Mihi the candle. "This tunnel will lead you back to the castle."

Then he picked the leather backpack off the floor and handed it to Reese. "And take this too. It can be scary out there, and you don't want to be caught hungry."

Mihi was pretty sure they'd never eat that porridge, but Reese nodded in thanks and tossed the bobby pins into the bag before swinging it over her shoulder.

"Farewell, Grey heroes." Blackberry bowed, and when he looked up again, Mihi saw a flash of determination. "Thank you for showing me that I can make my own way. That I can be better than my parents."

Mihi's heart squeezed, and the girls thanked him as they descended into darkness, taking the slippery, mold-soaked steps into the tunnel.

As Blackberry closed the trapdoor, he called out, "I should warn you: Don't change anything in the story. These stories have been the same for a long time. There's no telling what will happen if you change them now."

And then the door slammed shut, plunging them into darkness except for the flicker of Mihi's candle, which was quickly burning out.

"We'll be fine," Savannah said. "We won't change a thing."

Mihi swallowed. "Right."

As they stepped forward, Mihi heard a single word in the echo of their footsteps.

Heroes. Heroes. Heroes.

She turned Blackberry's word over in her mind, and it made her stand a little straighter. It made her feel a little braver.

She held that word close to her heart.

She would need it, with what they were about to face.

Chapter 26

They emerged from the tunnel to find Sleeping Beauty's castle completely covered by a maze of thick, black, thorny vines.

The thorn maze cast jagged shadows across Mihi's skin as she approached it, but she didn't feel afraid. She felt ready.

"Oh my," Savannah murmured. "These grew fast."

Reese picked up a stone and tossed it at the maze. The vines didn't budge. "At least the weeds don't seem to be moving anymore."

"Does this mean Sleeping Beauty's curse started?" Savannah asked.

Mihi squared her shoulders. "I don't know, but let's focus on finding the hidden door. In and out."

"We just have to find our way through this maze of terrifying plants that tried to kill us," Reese said,

hooking her thumbs under her backpack straps. "There must be a way, though. At some point, a prince has to find his way in."

Savannah bit her lip. "Yeah, but we aren't exactly princes."

"Nope," Mihi said. "We're better."

As they entered the menacing maze, Reese said, "This seems almost impossible."

The hairs on the back of Mihi's neck stood up. "*Almost.*"

"Hey!" Savannah peered in the vines and pulled something free. "My shoe!" she said, sliding it back onto her foot.

And then the three of them made their way into the maze, tracing and retracing their steps, wandering in and out of dead ends, ducking under and around twisted thorns—until, at last, they found the castle entrance.

"Finally," Savannah breathed.

With a sigh of relief, Mihi pulled open the grand doors. "We're home," she joked, only she was too afraid to joke, so it came off more panicked than funny.

Reese stopped. "What the . . . ?"

Mihi's breath caught as she stared at the grand ballroom.

Inside, members of the castle and all their royal guests were dressed in their finest clothing, dancing and twirling.

Only, the weird thing: They were all frozen.

Their expressions, their bodies, even their clothes were frozen in time, as if they were statues. They were just as frozen as the mural painted around them—that dreamy castle looming over this nightmare scene.

"This is so creepy," Savannah whispered.

Mihi walked up to one of the tuxedoed guests. She tapped his shoulder, but he didn't move. His skin was as cold and hard as marble.

The guests looked happy, frozen in laughter, eyes twinkling—but their happiness only made the scene creepier.

"Look at that," Savannah said.

Following her gaze, Mihi saw a wooden spinning wheel in the center of the ballroom, and Mihi knew for sure: Sleeping Beauty's curse had started. Mihi had hoped her gloves suggestion would work, but it clearly hadn't.

"The guests must have frozen when Sleeping Beauty fell asleep," Reese said.

But Savannah shook her head. "In the original fairy tale, aren't they supposed to fall asleep too?"

"Something's off," Mihi said. "We have to see if Sleeping Beauty's okay."

She sprinted up those gold stairs, taking them two at a time. Her friends ran after her, and the three of them burst into Sleeping Beauty's room.

There she was, asleep on her cloud of a bed, her blonde curls arranged around her face as if she were

floating. She lay peacefully, with her gloved hands resting on her stomach.

Gloved hands.

So Sleeping Beauty had listened to Mihi, but that hadn't saved her.

"I tried to help," Mihi murmured. "She told me she didn't want the curse

and the sleep and the kiss, so I told her to wear gloves.
I tried to help her change her ending."

Savannah's brows knit together as her eyes lingered
on the princess. "You did the best you could, but I
don't think princesses can change their stories."

"That's not the way this world works," Reese added.
"And you heard Bertha and Blackberry: Changing the
story is dangerous."

Mihi walked over to Sleeping Beauty's bed and sat
on the very edge. She knew they had to look for the
door—they had to escape this place as quickly as they
could. But seeing the princess like this woke a sadness
in Mihi.

"All I ever wanted was to be a princess," she said,
running a hand along Sleeping Beauty's soft, white
quilt, "and I got way too caught up in that. I thought
if I looked better or acted better, people would *see*
that in me. That I'd be . . . I don't know, special or
something. That I'd be the princess type."

Reese walked over and sat on the floor next to the
bed. "I get it, but we're never gonna look or act the
right way for some people. I mean, look at Bertha.
There was no pleasing her."

Savannah knelt beside Mihi and patted her knee. "It doesn't matter, though, because you're the princess type to us."

Mihi felt a tiny shift inside her, a small *click* in her heart. Because for the first time, she wondered what it even *meant* to be the princess type. Who got to decide that? This whole time, she'd been so worried about fitting in that she'd never thought to ask.

Mihi looked at her friends: Reese, with her curiosity and clever resourcefulness. Savannah, with her gentle kindness and bravery despite her fear. They felt like princesses to Mihi. Was that enough? Could your friends make up for the rest of the world?

Reese stood, offering her hand. "Let's go home."

Mihi nodded. "You're right. Let's find that door." She started to stand—but something wrapped around her wrist.

Reese's eyes popped and Savannah's hand flew to her mouth as they stared over Mihi's shoulder. Mihi whipped around to see Sleeping Beauty, hair a mess, eyes wide.

When the princess spoke, her voice cracked, and her fingers dug into Mihi's flesh. "Take me with you."

Chapter 27

"B ut—" Reese sputtered. "You're supposed to be enchanted!"

"I don't know what happened," Sleeping Beauty said, releasing Mihi's wrist. "I wore gloves during the ball, like Mihi said, and then I pricked my finger on that spinning wheel and fell asleep."

Savannah's brows pinched. "You were supposed to be asleep for much longer, until you were woken by a prince's kiss."

"I don't *want* a prince's kiss." She tilted her head. "Wait, how do you know the end of my story?"

"We're Greys," Mihi confessed. And she found she no longer felt embarrassed or annoyed or sad about that.

"Oh." Sleeping Beauty blinked. "I thought Greys only existed in stories."

Reese frowned. "Can I see your hands?"

Sleeping Beauty slid the gloves off, and Reese inspected her fingers. "The spinning wheel barely pricked your skin. You must have gotten a tiny dose of the enchantment, but not all of it."

Savannah looked at Mihi, eyes wide. "You really did make a difference."

Mihi's heart hiccupped. She'd done something good. She'd helped someone else. And that felt amazing. Even better than acting like a princess—she'd acted like a friend.

"But what now?" Savannah asked. "Wouldn't taking the princess away be changing the story? A lot?"

Sleeping Beauty considered this for a moment, then her eyes lit. She turned to Mihi. "You could trade places with me! I heard you talking about how you wanted to be a princess, and you *could*. You've trained for it! If *someone* was asleep here, waiting for their happily ever after, that might trick the magic of the realm."

Mihi thought about it. Could she really be the new Sleeping Beauty? Would that work?

She turned to her friends.

Savannah smiled sadly. "We want you to come with us. But if you decide to stay here longer . . . if that would make you happy . . . I understand."

Reese swallowed. "As long as you help us get home, we support you. You can stay behind." Then she hesitated before adding, "But I'll miss your wild brain."

Mihi let herself imagine it: *Royalty. Magic. A happily ever after.* No more questions about the world and where she fit inside it. Just an easy, simple, happy life. It was everything she'd ever wanted.

But . . . *did* she really want it? A life trapped in a castle, squeezing into someone else's idea of her? A life of ignoring other people's pain and hunger while she feasted? A life of . . . sleepwalking?

What if Mihi wanted more than a happily ever after? What if she wanted to change the world—and *keep* changing it? And what if she wanted to do that with her friends?

She shook her head. "I don't think that's my happily ever after, after all. I'm going with Reese and Savannah. I'm going home."

Savannah threw her arms around Mihi, and Mihi saw a smile grow on Reese's face.

When Savannah finally let go, Mihi said to Sleeping Beauty, "But you shouldn't be trapped here if you don't want to be."

She glanced at her friends, and they nodded.

"You can come with us," Reese said.

"You can change your story," Mihi added.

Sleeping Beauty paused. "Even if it's dangerous?"

Savannah nodded. "Even if it's dangerous."

"We've already survived Bertha, the Wood of Nightmares, and murderous bears," Reese added. "How much worse could it get?"

Sleeping Beauty smiled and slid out of bed. Her feet brushed the floor, and she stood.

They all held their breath, waiting for something, anything. But the castle was silent.

"I think it's safe—" Mihi started to say.

And then they heard a crash downstairs—followed by a moan.

Reese turned to the princess. "Do you know what that was?"

Sleeping Beauty shook her head.

They heard another series of crashes—and then the sound of hundreds of footsteps, scrambling up the staircase.

"Right," Savannah said. "This would be the danger part."

Before anyone could respond, the bedroom door flew open and Bertha burst through.

"Bertha!" Sleeping Beauty exclaimed.

But it didn't take long to realize that Bertha . . . wasn't *exactly* Bertha.

Because she was still half-frozen in her statue form—and though her lips stayed stuck in their happy-ballroom smile, her eyes roamed and rolled—searching, panicked. She leaned forward, stiff arms outstretched.

"*Princesssss*," she screeched, a scratching word forced through smiling lips.

The princess screamed. So did Mihi. And Reese. And Savannah.

Mihi grabbed a pillow and threw it at the head lady-in-waiting, but it bounced off, and Bertha hobbled forward, grasping for the girls.

Reese's voice shook. "I was wrong. It can get worse. It can definitely get worse."

They scrambled backward, pressing themselves against the wall as Bertha advanced.

They had changed this story.

And that was dangerous.

Chapter 28

"They're coming!" Reese shouted, pointing over Bertha's shoulder. "They're all coming."

Behind Bertha, a crowd of zombie-fied party guests advanced, completely blocking their only exit.

"What is *happening*?" Savannah yelped over the chaos. "They're like zombies!"

Bertha pulled at the princess's skirt, ripping off shreds of fabric, and the other ladies-in-waiting climbed over Bertha to get to the princess.

As Sleeping Beauty shrieked, Mihi fought them off with another useless pillow. "What do we do?" she gasped, as the zombie-statues ignored her feather-weight attacks.

"The window?" Savannah suggested.

The princess shook her head. "We're way too high."

Around them, the guests lurched forward, arms outstretched.

Mihi spun around, searching for a miraculous exit—and her eyes fell on the small food elevator Sleeping Beauty had shown her.

"The dumbwaiter!" she cried.

The princess's eyes grew wide and she ran toward it. "Get in!"

Mihi and her friends rushed over, but Reese bit her lip. "This doesn't look like it can hold four people. It's not even meant to hold *one* person."

"No time to worry about that now," Savannah said. She and the princess stuffed themselves inside first, followed by Reese, who was still wearing Blackberry's backpack.

There was no way Mihi would fit. "Reese," she said, as she dodged a lady-in-waiting, "take the backpack off!"

Reese squirmed, attempting to tug it off her shoulders, but she was wedged in tight. There was no time.

So Mihi took a deep breath and threw herself inside the tiny space, smashing against her friends.

The dumbwaiter creaked and groaned, and they were completely cramped, elbow to knee to shoulder. But the box held strong.

Sleeping Beauty jammed her finger against the down button, pressing, pressing, pressing. "Come on, come on, come on."

Slowly, oh so slowly, the doors began to close, but not before Bertha and the other ladies-in-waiting stuffed their hands through, grabbing at the girls' hair.

"The doors won't close!" Sleeping Beauty shouted.

Mihi, Reese, and Savannah pushed against those stiff hands, shoving them back, finger by cold finger, until finally, the doors slammed shut.

Chapter 29

As they began to descend, the dumbwaiter creaked, groaning under their combined weight.

"Please hold us," Savannah whispered.

In response, the box shuddered, shaking them so hard their teeth chattered.

"That didn't sound great," Reese said.

"The dumbwaiter wasn't built for this," Sleeping Beauty murmured.

"We'll be fine," Mihi insisted.

With that, they heard a *snap*—and the dumbwaiter began to free-fall.

Their screams echoed, and Mihi's stomach lifted and flipped like she was on a carnival ride without brakes.

"We're gonna DIE!" Savannah screamed.

As they gathered speed, Mihi thought she might be right.

Then they crashed to the floor, and their whole world shook. Mihi's brain rattled. But they were alive.

With Reese's help, she pried the doors open and the girls burst out, gasping for air.

"We survived," Mihi breathed.

"Against all laws of nature," Reese added.

"And it was kind of thrilling," Savannah said.

But they couldn't celebrate for long, because behind them they heard, "*Princesssssssss.*"

Sleeping Beauty winced. "Not again."

They turned to see Della, the head chef, and a butler, arms outstretched, just as Bertha and the party guests had been.

The head chef reached for Reese, who grabbed a brand-new wok off the stove and brandished it like a sword.

As the butler advanced on Mihi, Reese called, "Mihi, catch!" before tossing her a metal pot and a wooden spoon.

Mihi caught the cookware and fended the butler

off, just as a half-frozen Della lurched toward Savannah.

"Della, you were supposed to be our friend!" Savannah cried, shielding herself with a cupcake pan. "How do we stop this?"

Sleeping Beauty grabbed a basket of bread and started throwing rolls at the zombies. "The spinning wheel started this," she panted. "Maybe we have to destroy it."

Savannah held up her pan as Della backed her into a corner. "I'm trapped!"

"Hey, Della, over here!" Mihi cried, banging her spoon against the pot. Della turned and hobbled toward Mihi.

As she grasped for Mihi's hair, Mihi managed to block her with the spoon—but Della knocked it from her hand. Mihi held up the pot, but she knocked that away too.

Defenseless, Mihi looked to her friends for help, but they were all battling zombies of their own. Della inched closer, backing Mihi against the wall.

And then Mihi noticed the small bag of magic dust in Della's apron pocket.

If magic had gotten them into this mess, maybe it could get them out of it.

Mihi grabbed the bag of dust, dumped all of it onto her hands, and focused. She tried to think about the icing, but a plate in the corner of the room caught her eye. *Japchae.* The chef must have tested it.

Prickly magic flooded her, followed by the painful urge to sneeze. She fought it back and flicked her fingers, desperately trying to control the noodles as they lifted into the air. They wobbled. She was about to lose control.

Think of a happy memory. Mihi thought of dinnertime at home. Her mom stirring japchae noodles at the stove. Her dad chopping vegetables. Her brother sitting at the kitchen counter, talking about school. Her grandfather on the couch, watching TV. Her grandmother, finger-combing Mihi's hair as the scent of dinner filled the air.

Mihi swished her fingers, separating the noodles into three bunches, and moving them toward the butler, the head chef, and of course, Della.

She was so close—she just had to hang on a moment longer—and then she sneezed.

The japchae shot through the air, coating the zombies in a layer of potato starch noodles and fried veggies.

The zombies stumbled, unable to wipe the food from their eyes, and Mihi, Reese, and Savannah ducked and dodged.

"Let's go!" Sleeping Beauty shouted. "We have to get back to the ballroom."

Mihi turned to the princess just in time to see a party guest lurching up behind her, lunging for her head.

"Princess!" Mihi shouted. "Sugarplums!"

At the sound of the fainting code word, Sleeping Beauty dropped to the floor, and the guest leapt forward, snatching at the air where the princess's head had just been.

Sleeping Beauty hopped back to her feet, eyes wide. "Thanks."

"Follow me," Mihi called. She ran through the kitchen, ducking the zombies, clearing a path for her friends.

The girls exploded out of the kitchen, running

down the hall back toward the grand ballroom, toward the spinning wheel.

"We're almost there," Sleeping Beauty said.

But when they reached the ballroom entrance, Mihi pulled up short.

In front of them was the crowd of party guests.

Behind them were the noodle-covered zombies.

They were surrounded.

Chapter 30

"*P*rincesssss." The word echoed through the castle as the crowd spoke in unison.

They were trapped.

"We have to destroy the spinning wheel," Sleeping Beauty gulped.

"But *how?*" Reese cried.

Just past the party-guest zombies, Mihi could see the spinning wheel glowing in the center of the room, right under the gleaming chandelier. But there was no way through the crowd.

The four girls huddled together.

Mihi fought back tears. This was completely, utterly hopeless.

There was no way out. No happily ever after. No alternate fate. *This* was their ending.

Savannah reached for Mihi's hand. Reese reached for the other.

"We're in this together," Savannah whispered.

Mihi looked at her friends. Through their own tears, they nodded back at her, and Mihi felt brim-full with gratitude. They looked so brave, even now, as the zombies pushed in on them. Their eyes sparked with light, and the chandelier cast rainbows across their skin.

Mihi paused.

The chandelier.

She felt the familiar fizz of an idea.

The chandelier was held up by a single thread. It looked so fragile. Reese was right. It seemed impossible.

Mihi's gaze fell to the spinning wheel, just below the chandelier.

"Reese," she said. "Give me the backpack."

Reese frowned. "What? Now?"

But Mihi didn't have time to explain. She took the backpack, closed one eye, and aimed.

The bag left her hands—arcing up, up, up, slicing through the air as if in slow motion.

As Mihi watched it fly, her stomach flipped. The chandelier was so *high*. Her aim was so *bad*.

This wouldn't, couldn't, shouldn't work.

Except—somehow—the bag hit the chandelier with a *ping*.

Not too hard. Maybe not hard enough.

But that poor chandelier swayed back and forth, and that single thread began to fray.

The bag fell back down, hitting the ballroom floor with a thud, and the girls watched the chandelier swaying, swaying.

Cold fingers brushed against their skin. The zombies were so close.

And then, with a thunderous roar, the chandelier broke from the ceiling and crashed to the floor, right onto the spinning wheel.

The girls ducked, shielding themselves as bits of glass and wood exploded in every direction.

And just like that, the zombies collapsed, snoring, fast asleep.

✧Chapter 31✧

ertha woke first, pushing herself up from the ground. Her tight bun had unraveled, but she looked just as annoyed as ever. "What happened? Princess, are you okay?"

Sleeping Beauty nodded. "I'm more than okay, thanks to my friends."

Bertha looked between Mihi, Reese, and Savannah and shook her head. "I was supposed to say something to you three. Or . . . do something. But my memory's a little fuzzy. Everything feels like a dream."

She rubbed her head. "I need to make myself a cup of tea. I'll deal with you three later."

Mihi shuddered. She would *not* miss Bertha.

As Bertha walked off to the kitchen and other castle guests and staff began to wake, Sleeping Beauty pulled the girls aside.

"I'm sorry for messing everything up for you," Mihi said.

"Are you kidding me?" Sleeping Beauty said. "You saved me from mortal danger."

"But I was the one who caused that danger by telling you to wear gloves," Mihi said.

"First of all," Sleeping Beauty responded, "you didn't cause that danger. A jealous fairy did. Because I live in a terrifying world.

"And second of all," she continued, "you three showed me that the world doesn't have to be the way I thought it did. And *I* don't have to be the way I thought I did. You saved me from my own ladies-in-waiting, gave me a wild adventure, and changed my life. You're *heroes*."

Mihi's throat hurt as feeling rose up, threatening to spill over. "You know, you can still come with us, if you want."

"Our world is far from perfect," Reese added. "Some people still judge you based on how you look. But when you have the right friends, it feels a little easier."

Mihi's heart pinched for Reese—her compassionate, brilliant friend.

"Thanks," Sleeping Beauty said. "But I'm going to stay here and take care of my castle. Because of you, I realized I have a lot more power than I thought. Now that I know there's another way, maybe I can help change my world. Princesses shouldn't have to live locked away in a castle. Ladies-in-waiting shouldn't have to spend their lives taking care of me. Everyone deserves a chance to live their own dreams. *That's* what I want my kingdom to look like."

Savannah beamed at the princess. "That's amazing," she said. "I know you can do it."

Sleeping Beauty blushed at the compliment, then turned to Mihi. "You could stay with me. You could help me make the Rainbow Realm better."

Mihi felt her heart reaching toward the idea. Together, the four of them had made it through the dark side of the story and changed it for the better. They'd done something Bertha said they never could.

And Mihi couldn't deny that despite the danger, she still loved this place, with its magic and the characters she'd grown up loving.

But the other part of her heart tugged too. The part

that missed her family. The part that loved her friends. The part that wondered if maybe her world had big changes to make too.

"I need to go home," she said. As the words left her mouth, she knew it was the right choice. But she also felt, in a quiet part of her, like this wasn't the last time she'd see this magical world.

Sleeping Beauty walked over to pick up the backpack and handed it to Reese before hugging them goodbye. Then she left to take care of her waking party guests.

"Time to go home," Savannah said.

"We just have to figure out how," Reese added.

Mihi felt a whirring in her pocket, and when she reached inside, she realized it was the compass. She pulled out the metal object and opened it to see that the arrow was pointing directly to the mural on the wall.

Mihi looked up at that painting of a castle—with painted castle doors. And right below it, the words, *Home is where the heart is.*

"What if . . . ?" she whispered.

Her friends followed her gaze from the compass to the mural.

"The painting?" Savannah asked.

Reese tilted her head. "The refrigerator didn't look like a portal either."

"Do you think the compass points to the portal doors?" Mihi asked quietly.

Reese frowned. "Where'd you say you got that thing?"

"I don't know. I found it in my pocket after we left the castle, but I don't know how it got there."

"Maybe someone was on our side after all," Savannah said.

It could've been the princess, the cooks, Della. Or maybe it was one of the ladies-in-waiting, or a seamstress, like Reese had originally suggested. It could have been anyone.

"Either way," Reese said, "we still need a way to activate it. When we came through, we needed the candy to see through the other side."

With blooming despair, Mihi realized, "But we don't have any candy."

HOME IS WHERE THE HEART IS

Savannah looked like she might cry. Reese swallowed hard.

And then, a memory nudged at Mihi's mind. "The bear's porridge . . . it reminded me of rice cakes."

Reese's eyes widened as she followed Mihi's train of thought. "And it reminded me of buttercream. And, Sav, you said it tasted like beef jerky."

Savannah's hand flew to her mouth. "The same way the candies tasted."

Reese nodded. "Like home."

"The black bear did say homesickness was powerful magic, in small doses," Mihi said.

"And we have a small dose of it." Reese pulled the thermos full of porridge out of her backpack.

Savannah tugged at her hair. "What if this doesn't work?"

"It's worth a shot," Mihi said. "But I'll take a bite first, in case something goes wrong."

Reese shook her head. "I'm doing it with you. We survived this far—what's a tiny bite of porridge?"

"Reese, stop jinxing us!" Savannah said. "Okay. We do this together."

So together, they each took a bite.

As soon as the porridge passed their lips, the mural shimmered and swirled. Before their eyes, those painted castle doors opened up—revealing a pathway to their school library.

"We were right!" Reese said.

Mihi took one final look at the castle—at the ball-gowned guests and the princess helping them up. This had been Mihi's dream for so long—a dream she never thought was possible.

Despite needing to go home, despite *wanting* to go home, Mihi couldn't help but feel a small pinprick of sadness. "Goodbye," she whispered.

Then, linking arms, the girls stepped forward and walked through the doors, leaving the fairy tale behind.

Chapter 32

The world shimmered around them like a popped bubble, and they fell forward, landing face-first on the library floor. Behind them, the refrigerator blew its cold breath onto their backs. Above them, the wall clock ticked. Only a few minutes had passed.

Savannah jumped up, spinning around. "We're here. We made it. We're home." Then she dropped back to her knees and kissed the floor.

Reese stood, looking down at herself. Like Mihi and Savannah, she wore the same clothes she had when they'd left their world. Gone were the ripped and muddied ball gowns. But when Mihi stuck her hand into her pants pocket, her fingers brushed against cold silver. Somehow, the compass had traveled with her.

She pushed it deeper into her pocket. She'd worry about that later.

Reese examined the refrigerator—which now looked like any old appliance. This time, though, she kept a careful distance.

Mihi stood up, gently closing the refrigerator door. "We can keep that shut for a while."

Down the library hall, they heard voices, and the girls turned to one another.

"Ms. Lavender's back," Savannah said.

"Act like nothing happened," Mihi added.

They hurried out of the lounge and back to the front desk, acting as casual as possible.

And there was Genevieve, returning a stack of books to Ms. Lavender. Most of the books were contemporary novels, books about real kids in the real world, without a trace of magic. But at the very bottom was a brightly colored book—a story about princesses in fairy-tale lands.

When Genevieve looked up at Mihi and her friends, she shoved that book aside, trying to hide it.

"It's okay to like fairy tales," Mihi said, searching her former friend for some kind of sign—anything to prove she still cared.

"They're pretty interesting," Reese added.

"And they're starting to change," Savannah said.

Genevieve sniffed. "I *don't* like them. Fairy tales are for little kids. I'm not like *you*, Mihi." She pushed the books into Ms. Lavender's hands and huffed out of the library.

Mihi sighed. She would never understand Genevieve, but Mihi found, to her surprise, that Genevieve's words didn't bother her anymore.

Ms. Lavender tilted her head, a strange expression on her face. "Are they? Starting to change?"

"Uh . . ." Reese said.

"We just love hearing new stories," Mihi said, "and new adventures."

For a moment, Mihi got the tingling feeling that Ms. Lavender *knew*. But then the odd look on their librarian's face cleared, and she smiled. "Yes, of course. Now you three get settled. I'm sure you can find some good books to read during recess."

"We will," Savannah said. "Thanks, Ms. L."

As they walked away from Ms. Lavender, through the library stacks, Reese said, "We still have all of indoor recess left. What do we do now?"

Savannah laughed. "Kiss the floor a million more times?"

The girls found a cluster of beanbags in the corner and sank into them, whispering about their adventures, wondering, even now, how any of that had happened.

All Mihi Whan Park had ever wanted was to be a princess. She'd spent so much time and energy trying to fit in, trying to be good enough. But everything had changed. *She* had changed.

What was she supposed to want now? Despite all the chaos, that magical door still tugged at her, that call for adventure.

So many questions hung in the air, unanswered. What would happen to Sleeping Beauty's castle now? Had the orchard girl really been Snow White's evil queen? And what about Goldilocks—had she really been a Grey?

And, of course, there was that compass, heavy in her pocket. Where had it come from? Who had given it to her? And what other secrets did that world hold?

Mihi hoped she'd get her answers one day. But as she watched her new friends laughing together, telling and retelling their story, she decided: She was ready to leave her dream of being a princess in the past. Because she could be special, even if she wasn't a princess. She could be a hero, even without talking bears and zombie ladies-in-waiting.

And she wasn't alone. She had Reese. She had Savannah. And they were happy, but this wasn't their happily ever after. Their story would keep growing.

Credits

MARKETING + PUBLICITY

Leigh Ann Higgins . . . . *Marketing*
Mariel Dawson. . . . . *Marketing*
Melissa Zar . . . . *Marketing*
Mary Van Akin . . . . *School & Library Marketing*
Chantal Gersh . . . . *Publicity*
Brittany Pearlman. . . . . *Publicity*
Molly Ellis . . . . *Publicity*
Jen Edwards . . . . *Sales*

REPRESENTATION

Faye Bender . . . . *Literary Agent*
Jasmine Lake. . . . . *Film Agent*

Don't miss Mihi and her friends' next adventure

A GIANT PROBLEM

Coming Summer 2023

Mihi bubbled with joy. Savannah and Reese had given up recess! To hang out with *her* in the library! "You two are the best," she told them. Then she leaned forward. "Genevieve was here, which was kind of terrible, but she didn't . . . She decided to sit at the front of the library."

Savannah tilted her head. "I didn't see her when we walked in."

"I got a weird feeling when we talked to Ms. Lavender, though," Reese added, lowering her voice. "I think she knows about the portal. And I think she knows we went through it."

"Really?" Mihi asked. The hairs on the back of her neck prickled. "But . . . it doesn't matter, right? Because you don't want to go back?" Mihi tried not to sound too hopeful.

"Oh," Reese said. "Well, yeah. I guess that's a good point."

Mihi ducked her head to hide her disappointment. But something nagged at her. "You didn't see Genevieve at all?"

Savannah shrugged. "Maybe she went to the bathroom or something."

Mihi nodded, but worry rolled through her stomach. "I'll be right back," she blurted, pushing out of her chair and speed-walking down the hallway.

Surely, everything was fine. Surely, Mihi was being paranoid.

She turned the corner into the librarian's lounge—and there, sitting on the floor next to the wide-open refrigerator, was Genevieve's backpack.